SO-AVP-760

Sharon Butala

Season of Fury and Wonder

and Wonder

short stories

COTEAU
BOOKS

© Sharon Butala, 2018

All rights reserved. No part of this publication may be reproduced, stored in a retrieval system or transmitted, in any form or by any means, without the prior written consent of the publisher or a licence from The Canadian Copyright Licensing Agency (Access Copyright). For an Access Copyright licence, visit www.accesscopyright.ca or call toll free to 1-800-893-5777.

These stories are works of fiction. Names, characters, businesses, places, events and incidents are either the product of the author's imagination or used in a fictitious manner. Any resemblance to actual persons, living or dead, or actual events is purely coincidental.

Edited by Dave Margoshes
Book designed by Grace Cheong
Typeset by Susan Buck
Printed and bound in Canada

Library and Archives Canada Cataloguing in Publication

Butala, Sharon, 1940-, author
    Season of fury and wonder : short stories / Sharon Butala.

Issued in print and electronic formats.
ISBN 978-1-55050-974-8 (softcover).--ISBN 978-1-55050-975-5 (PDF).--
ISBN 978-1-55050-976-2 (EPUB).--ISBN 978-1-55050-977-9 (Kindle)

    I. Title.

PS8553.U6967S43 2019   C813'.54   C2018-905280-5
                                                 C2018-905281-3

2517 Victoria Avenue
Regina, Saskatchewan
Canada S4P 0T2
www.coteaubooks.com

Available in Canada from:
Publishers Group Canada
2440 Viking Way
Richmond, British Columbia
Canada V6V 1N2

10 9 8 7 6 5 4 3 2 1

Coteau Books gratefully acknowledges the financial support of its publishing program by: the Saskatchewan Arts Board, The Canada Council for the Arts, the Government of Saskatchewan through Creative Saskatchewan, the City of Regina. We further acknowledge the [financial] support of the Government of Canada. Nous reconnaissons l'appui [financier] du gouvernement du Canada.

 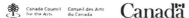

*To the old women
who have shaped the world*

Table of Contents

Preface

These stories are about old women. I wanted to make them about old women's lives *now*, as they live them, and not stories about their pasts as most writers have done, but I found, as I wrote, that inevitably the past interfered, popped up, refused to be batted down, and I had to accept that the past is very much an integral part of the *now* for all old people. If old age is a time of re-ordering the past, often of re-understanding it, of discovery, of trying to draw a clear narrative line through it, of finding, at last, recurring or steady themes, and of summing up – all of which it definitely is, at least among the wise – then reflection, musing, meditating on the past is inevitable, and very much to be desired. The *now*, it turns out, only makes sense in terms of the past.

As one's world draws in, gets smaller and smaller, the inner life grows stronger and deeper. Life becomes thought. The grave danger is letting thought become dream, illusion, delusion, hallucination. This detachment from reality happens (when, of course, it is not caused by a disease) when the old person lives alone, or sees only other, younger, adults who have no respect for the aged person as a human being.

Around mid-September 2016, I woke with an entire short story in my head, or perhaps my 'head' is not where it was at all, but in some space I reach only once in a long while when I'm *not-thinking* about a writing project. This wasn't a dream; I just woke up, went to my computer, and didn't stop writing until the full story was on the page. I'd never written a short story this way before in my life, although I'd written many stories and published three collections of them, and I was, if not exactly surprised by this manifestation of creativity, quite simply in awe of it.

Almost immediately a second short story followed, more or less by the same route. Then in the night I heard the words, "Three Sisters", and I had a third short story that came as easily to me as the other two.

In the fourteen years since my last collection, *Real Life*, I hadn't written a single short story and didn't believe that I would ever write one again. But in my nights when I had been sleeping and the short stories appeared inside me, an idea I had never formulated (at least, not in waking life) had come with them. The first story worked, I thought, as a response to Raymond Carver's famous "What We Talk

About When We Talk About Love." Immediately after finishing the story, I began looking for a title. I knew the story was about love, and thought at once that it was about another way of looking at love than in Carver's story, which I had taught not long before. And with a sense of my own audacity, I decided to call my story "What *Else* We Talk About When We Talk About Love."

That triggered the thought of writing a series of stories, *each one in response to, or inspired by, or a riff on,* (never a copy of or an attempt to copy) one of the short stories by other, mostly earlier, writers whose work I was taught in the fifties and early sixties at the University of Saskatchewan, which were the 'great' stories. This device thrilled me, and a half-dozen of these stories came flooding over me so fast that I had to type each idea quickly and then temporarily abandon it in order to write the next one before I lost it. In three months and a bit, I had ten new short stories in my computer, over forty thousand words. I kept on revising and organizing and one day I sat down to write this explanation.

One of the greatest benefits of my following this inspiration was that I had the immense pleasure of re-reading many of these 'great' stories: Carver's "What We Talk About When We Talk About Love," (published in 1981 many years after I left university), James Joyce's "The Dead," Flannery O'Connor's "A Good Man is Hard to Find," Shirley Jackson's "The Lottery," Willa Cather's "Paul's Case" (which, although still relevant, I find almost nobody remembers), John Cheever's "The Swimmer," Alan Sillitoe's "The Loneliness of the Long Distance Runner," Hemingway's "Hills Like White Elephants," Tim O'Brien's "The Things They Carried," (not published until about 1990), and two that didn't come from short stories at all, but from Edgar Allan Poe's poem, "The Raven," and Chekhov's play, "Three Sisters."

This collection of short stories is a soul-felt tribute to those writers, to their immense creativity, wisdom, and art, which has enriched all our lives and helped to carry the species forward just a little. My gratitude to them is unending. The opportunity to explore what I know about being old was as exciting as learning to walk as a small child, or first moving away from my family as a young adult, must have been.

—*Sharon Butala, Calgary, May 2018*

WHAT *ELSE* WE TALK ABOUT WHEN WE TALK ABOUT LOVE

Inspired by Raymond Carver's "What We Talk About When We Talk About Love",
1981

WHEN MY SISTER JAIMIE'S HUSBAND WAS CLOSE TO DEATH I WENT TO the city where they lived to see him. My three brothers and two other sisters and I had been emailing each other for some time, occasionally phoning – we are too old, the bunch of us, to text, or tweet or whatever, we find these methods of communication insulting – so when their two diagnoses of cancer finally came, none of us was surprised. A collective silence held across the provinces in our different houses, each of us looking out our windows at our own landscapes – city, ocean, forest – each of us trying desperately to think, as if thinking could solve what wasn't even properly a problem, or that we might thereby enter a new dimension where the news would be ordinary and reasonable, and out of which we could decide how to behave, and what attitude to take that would be natural and obvious.

I said "collective silence," but it isn't quite the right description of what each of us felt. I think to express whatever it was, in our newly truncated conversations, we must have resorted to clichés like *we were stunned into silence*, because the real words for what we felt were not forthcoming just then, or, more sensibly, we did not yet know what we felt beyond – would it be right to say that we were simply *aghast?* Or is that just another cliché? And it wasn't as if we weren't familiar with cancer; we were all too familiar with it in its various forms, and it was true that on the day the diagnoses finally came more of our family members with cancer – aunts, cousins, our parents, a grandparent – had died than had survived. Only one survived, actually. We had to have hoped that these two who were so close to us would both survive as well, but I think that every one of us knew in our heart of hearts that they weren't going to make it, either. Don't ask me how we knew that. The universe at work, I suppose, the knowledge hanging in the air for the plucking, and us trying to ignore it, stubbornly refusing it.

For a long time I had wanted to be a decent person, actually tried to figure out how one would go about achieving this goal. I suppose that sounds silly as I'm guessing that every liberal, well-ed-ucated, good-hearted person knows how to do that. But I don't think it was ever obvious to me. My earliest contact with such an idea just came back to me now – me telling a girl famous for being the nicest person in our high school crowd that I thought being nice was too stupid for words. I was maybe seventeen and had no idea what I was trying to say, but it is clear to me now that I wanted to hurt her, because I could not figure out how anyone could stand to be 'nice.' I couldn't manage it. I recall that I felt too furious when I tried, trying enraged me, and I undermined my own effort imme-diately by saying or doing something we would have called 'mean.' I think that even as a kid I thought there were more interesting and important things to be than nice (even though I had no idea what they were), and even though being nice was considered to be the most important thing anybody in our teenaged world could be.

Now, knowing our brother-in-law was the sicker of the two and hadn't much time left, and even though I had never liked him much, it seemed clear that decency required that I visit him. Jaimie and her husband Austen had been married for many years, had married so young that they had been married longer than I, the eldest of our seven siblings, had. They had four children and many grand-children and even a great-grandchild, with another one on the way, even though they were only in their mid-sixties. We knew too, that, as with many long-married couples, they loved each other deeply, while at the same time hating each other, and would never in life part. In my experience, having been married and divorced twice, all the wretched drama of my marriages and divorces having ended years ago now, and yet still alternately loving and hating each of my husbands (when I think about them at all), I can only suppose these emotions were just like most long-married people's. (But I'm getting whimsical, a growing fault of mine that my aging children, looking at me sideways, clearly connect to dementia.)

We loved our sister, but we didn't love her husband, and some of us, probably unfairly, outright disliked him. Most of us dealt with him by carefully maintaining an even front, while others could barely do that and instead chose to stay away. Our youngest sister's marriage all those years ago had brought the only real breach in our family's long agreeable relations, which, if they weren't exactly love, consisted of mutual loyalty, based no doubt on not much more than our individual need to feel we belonged somewhere, and somewhere that we might think of as a foundation in our lives. But I find it so odd how people don't know what other people think of them, preferring instead to think that if they aren't quite loved, they are at least liked, and their worst faults, which they try to keep hidden even from themselves, haven't been noticed, or have been accepted as harmless. But I am referring to my sister's husband, who didn't love us, didn't even like us much, who must have blamed us for things – whatever things they were – just as we tended to blame him. And yet, I am fairly sure that for all our years together as family, Austen didn't even register the fact that we didn't like him.

If the pathos of this new situation didn't escape any of us, it also didn't escape the doctors or the nurses, or anyone else who came in contact with Jaimie and Austen during the long period of their dying. So there was much kindness from strangers, whether medical or not, and a dearth of talk among the rest of us because this situation was too unfathomably diabolical to find words for. Not even we – well-educated, well-read, sympathetic white liberals with the requisite good hearts, and proper attitudes – could speak about it beyond platitudes and what medical jargon we were privy to and sometimes puzzled over with each other.

I longed to see my sister, and to hold her as our mother would have done had she been alive (our mother's was the first cancer death – no, sorry, it was the second), but Jaimie was surrounded by her own family to whom she was wife, mother, grandmother, and they were a private, closed bunch who didn't want to allow a sister any right to be intimately involved in her dying. My sister's family and my siblings all knew that I wouldn't attempt intimacy in the dying of her husband, so that was never an issue; in fact, nobody paid any attention to my visit where he was concerned, and this even though I had come to see him, to say what I had no doubt would be good-bye forever. You might wonder why I would bother.

But what could I say to a dying man I didn't love, mostly didn't even like, who had been a part of my life, albeit at a distance, all my adulthood, who was related to me, whose children had my blood in their veins, and who, in a hugely complicated ball of feelings was hated but mostly loved by my sister who was herself dying? How could I be fully honest, genuine in my sympathy? Or should I be thinking of empathy? Or, heaven forgive me, their lofty relation, compassion? (Let's just say I took it for granted he didn't like me, although he didn't actively dislike me, but frankly, I'm sure he couldn't care less if I lived or died.) I could truly say, as I sat crowded into the centre seat on the plane, that I wanted to be fully touched by his dying, that I wanted to understand at the deepest level that his life had not been an easy one, that bad things had happened to him, as they happen to all of us, which had helped to make him who he was; that I knew he had some very good qualities, and that I knew I had to recognize that he deserved every bit of sympathy, empathy, or compassion that I could muster. That, finally, in the end – and this was the end – whether I liked him or not or he me just plain didn't matter anymore.

And, of course, I had to consider my sister. To hurt him in this situation would deal a blow to her that she might be unable to bear. So I knew, absolutely, that I had to find a way to be with him that would hurt no one and yet would feel genuine to me. And also knowing all the while that if I tried to tell anyone what I was feeling and thinking about this visit, they would simply decide that I'd lost my mind, or that, as usual, I was being a selfish pig who thought only of myself. This point is where I always lose the sense of the worthwhileness of thinking about one's responsibility or one's guilt – that it is worth the effort. It isn't worth the effort, there is no end, there is no bloody end to it, just the infamous rabbit hole that you, I, everyone, ends up disappearing down. So, should I fake it? Just what would that consist of? Pretending that I cared? But I wouldn't be pretending; I did care. Just not the way a person who loved him would care.

The truth is, I am not a person who is any good at loving. Although I try, I am famously cold. I don't hug people when I meet them or say good-bye to them, not even people I like very much. I don't watch movies about love – shudder at the very thought – or sing any of those appalling love songs, or admire lovesickness or think it is cute or touching. I don't ever talk about love, I don't even fully believe that there is such a thing as love. (I exclude from that belief parent-child love. I do believe in that. And I guess that I have to admit that apparently I believe siblings can love each other, at least now and then, for a while.)

My strange inability to love may have begun when I was a small child in catechism class, where I was taught it was a terrible sin not to love God, and I knew I was condemned to hell forever because I couldn't love God, who seemed to me – not that I ever dared at the time to even think it – a monster of the most terrifying, indeed, unimaginable proportions. No, it was more the result of finally, as a young woman, admitting that I alone of my brothers and sisters was not loved by my mother. But I will not bore you with that; nowadays, having thought it through, it bores me to death, too. I'm trying, as an old woman, to shift my sympathy, empathy, compassion, from me to her, who had her own difficulties that had warped her and who, I see now, was suffering terribly while we were living through our childhoods.

No one met me at the airport, which was a relief to me (I am also something of a loner), and I went straight to my hotel, having refused all offers from family members of a bed because I knew their households were crowded enough as they were, and that they were also full of pity, confusion, and concern, without having to deal with me, too. It didn't surprise me either that no one protested my decision, or protested it only in a strictly *pro forma* way. That was a relief too.

Anyway, as I kept telling myself, I've been through so much worse than this situation in my life (I refused to enumerate what these 'worse' situations might be), and if I am ever to figure out what this elusive 'being nice, being decent' thing really is, I have got to do this. I have got to do this right.

About an hour after I'd checked in and left my overnight bag in my hotel room, my taxi pulled up in front of the house which, after years of moving around, my sister and her husband had settled into. A home-care person was there when I arrived and she made a pot of tea and served it to my sister, still well enough to walk around the house and chat for a while, to me and to a couple of other more distant family members, second cousins, who drank their tea quickly, and left. Alone, our chat consisted of a cursory inventory of her symptoms, a faintly horrified review of the last, worst one, which a new medication had at least temporarily taken care of, and a series of fraught silences, which began with sentences one or the other of us started but chose not to end, or couldn't end, accompanied usually by gazes too profound to be called merely sad, into space, quickly broken by one or the other of us with a new, inconsequential comment in a carefully light tone. For instance, my sister said, "Auntie Daisy and Lily came a few days ago."

"Oh," I said. "I haven't seen either of them in years. How is Lily?" Lily has suffered from severe depression since she was a teenager.

"Beth Billings was here too." They had gone to high school together. "A day or two ago? I think, maybe..."

"Maybe?" I prompted, but my sister didn't seem to hear me.

"Have you seen my box of tissue? Where is it?" The home-care person, who appeared to be busy in the kitchen and paying no attention to us, unobtrusively and silently picked the box off the sideboard and set it on my sister's knees. Jaimie appeared not to notice. She didn't touch the tissues.

"How long has Austen been back from the hospital?"

"Mmm," she said. She turned her head toward the home-care lady who was back in the kitchen.

"A few days," the woman called. "Five days."

We talked about her hospitalization, and the ensuing release, about her and her husband's various medical tests and procedures, and plans as to how to manage what would happen next. But this last was mostly about what would happen next to her husband, who was at this point bedridden, although not yet in the hospital or a hospice, but who could not get up even for the bathroom without a couple of people helping him.

I cannot say what I felt during all of this uneasy, non-communication. We had been taught by our mother to save our tears or any other strong emotion except laughter for when we were alone, that to 'break down' in public was shameful, so mostly none of us did. It was really very odd behavior, I see now, but it came out of, I

6

think, that British stiff-upper-lip nonsense. Our father's family, Latin all the way, held no such compunction; its members were, if anything, far too emotional for anybody's good, or so our mother had taught us to think. I have personally discovered over the years, and especially since our mother has been long dead, that if you constantly stifle your feelings out of concern for what you have been taught is appropriate behavior, you soon can't feel anything at all. Or at least, you have to dig very deep to figure out what your real feelings are, and that mostly this will not seem worth the trouble of doing.

Eventually, I could see that my sister was having difficulty sitting upright, or smiling naturally, and being engaged in our conversation. I understood that it was time to go, and I could only hope that I would be able to return to see her at least one more time before her illness reduced her to a shell who wouldn't even know me when I visited. I remembered then that I had come to see her husband whose illness was far advanced on hers, a purpose that the moment I saw her in the flesh I had completely forgotten. Now I saw that this had always been a poorly considered undertaking, and thinking of what lay in the moments ahead, I was briefly afraid, and might have left without seeing him.

But she said then, "Don't go without saying good-bye to Austen." I nodded and smiled and the home-care worker and I helped her to her feet and walked her down the hall to the master bedroom where her husband was lying in the queen-sized bed under the stylishly-patterned duvet. My sister always did have wonderful taste, and the design and colour of the duvet fit perfectly into the décor of this handsome, if small, bedroom. My sister made her own way down the left side of the bed and perched on it, her legs curled under her, beside her husband who lay in shadow beside her. Behind us we could hear the home-care worker returning down the hall to the kitchen. I remained standing just inside the doorway while Jaimie settled herself, and until my eyes adjusted to the relative darkness at that end of the room so that I could make out Austen's face. The duvet was pulled up under his chin and he didn't move except to pull one hand slowly out from under the cover.

In a weak voice, he said, "I'm sorry I can't get up to...." I think he meant to hug me, or shake my hand as a gentleman would. We were both deeply embarrassed – I believe that's what it was – but, if so, it now seems a peculiar reaction on both our parts.

"Don't even think of such a thing," I said. "I don't want to disturb you. I only came to say hello before I go."

I could think of no way to say that I hoped he was doing all right, or that he wasn't in pain, or was managing, or whatever. Perhaps how sorry I was that such a thing was happening, but I knew I could never say that, although I found at that moment that this was more true than anything I had ever said to anyone in my life, or failed to say, but had thought. I could not say a word more than that I had come to say "hi" before I left. But then I thought that this was one time when I needed to hug him, to kiss his cheek – no, that the situation required this.

In the gloom of that room, with my dying sister beside him, lounging tentatively against the pillows that she had pulled up to support her back, as if at any second she might have to leap up and do something or other, smiling nervously at me, and he – could he have been near tears? I couldn't see well enough to tell – I was about to move down the side of the bed to his head so that I could try to hold him briefly and could kiss him, perhaps, I thought, on his forehead, when swiftly, the room filled up with love.

I knew that although it did not emanate from me as I did not love him, it seemed to be coming through me; I was its conduit. Although I, too, was permeated with it, it was not that I suddenly, personally, now loved him. Also, astonishingly, I could actually see the love that had come and filled the room. The odd thing is that whenever I try to tell people this story – very seldom, I assure you – nobody ever asks me what love looked like. Ahhh. What to say. It was a dusky beige-pink; it had a very fine, soft, pebbly texture; it was very still, there was such beauty in that stillness; it gave the impression of perhaps – I'm being careful here – being maybe alive itself. But I might be adding that last because that is what people would say, of course. God in his goodness, and all that. That, instead, perhaps that exquisitely beautiful stillness, that very *presence*, was enough and the truest thing about it. Its *thing-ness*. An essence in itself.

My sister saw or felt it; she made a kind of inadvertent, gentle-sounding and surprised "ohh," and her husband did something the same, "mmm" perhaps, close to a mild grunt, so he too felt or saw it, or both. Even in my awe and surprise or whatever it was I was feeling, I kept on moving down the side of the bed, and when I reached his head, bent to hold him and to kiss his forehead. As I was placing my hands gently on each shoulder, he said again, "I'm sorry

I can't get up," again seeming to mean so as to respond courteously. In the midst of this, the love that was not exactly mine remained. But I held his shoulders briefly, lightly, and kissed his forehead as I had planned, murmured a few words that I can't remember, including probably that I was flying back home the next morning. As I left the room, I think, the love had dissipated or had departed. It was all so much; I couldn't – I can't – remember details. I don't think my sister left the bed. I believe I walked out alone. I must have come down the hall so silently that the home-care worker, still in the kitchen, didn't hear me and didn't say good-bye.

Indeed, although I did return several times in order to see my sister as her condition worsened, and although her husband lived weeks longer in a hospice, I never saw him again and, yet again, I did not know how to feel about this. It would be mawkish to say that thinking about it makes my chest ache, that it is as if there is a large burr or something in back of my forehead.

How could it be, I ask myself again and again, that I, who was not good at loving, who had had to teach myself to be decent, and who did not love that man, could have been a channel for some sort of disembodied or disconnected love to come and fill that room so full of the crushing, mindless cruelty that afflicts all human life and that could, for an instant at least, overcome the horror of the world? I am not sure if that is even true – overcoming the horror of the world. No, I cannot allow that thought; it is utterly sentimental.

I think my wonderment was that love had come alone, unasked for, unwilled, unexpected; the wonder was that it could exist in such a way, all by itself. But I've said that. The wonder is that the three of us saw it, felt it, and two of us then died, and only I am left who knows that such a thing can happen, and am trying, in these last few years, to alter my understanding to encompass it.

GRACE'S GARDEN

Inspired by Alan Sillitoe's, "The Loneliness of the Long Distance Runner", 1959

As Grace advanced through the hallway's gloom, she could see a man pressing his face against the lead-seamed stained-glass beside the front door. When he saw her, he dropped the hand he had been cupping beside his eye, and stepped back. Clearly, she thought, Steven had warned him she might not answer the door, although she was always at home. No use, she would have to let him in.

"Hi, Mrs. Mercer." He offered a cautious smile. "I'm Everett Gower, pastor at the Plains of Hope Church."

"I know who you are," she told him briskly, although the croak in her voice made her sound a good deal more uncertain than she had intended. She stood back to let him pass into the hall, but, as he was half-way through, lost her grip on the heavy oak door so that it hit him on the shoulder and upper arm. "So sorry," she said, although, of course, she wasn't. She saw no reason to put up with his visit, except that here she was, putting up with it.

The kitchen, where she took him, had once been filled with sunlight when the children were little and Reuben was alive. Now the dying elms crowded out most of the light, and the tall stocks of pink or blue hollyhocks that used to nod and wink at her above the window sills – her father had planted them when she was a child – had, without good light, long ago died out. Puzzled, she noticed that his eyes had widened, turned in the direction of his gaze and saw that a burner on the gas stove was blazing away.

"I turned that on to make tea just as I heard your ring at the door," she said, trying not to sound defensive. In fact, she had no memory of turning it on, but if she couldn't explain that flame burning away without even a kettle on it, Steven would have the city on her in a minute and would force her into signing that damn power of attorney, and she would be finished. Hurriedly, which, she recognized, was actually glacially slowly, she pulled the kettle – thank god it was full, although who had filled it? and when? – over the flame. She now kept the few utensils and dishes – a plate, a bowl, two cups, a water glass – she used all the time on the counter within easy reach.

She carried the pair of saucerless cups to the table where Pastor What's-His-Name was sitting with a hint of tension in his shoulders and a self-righteous smile on his mouth. His eyes were tiny, light blue, and hard, his pupils so contracted they had virtually disappeared. Where the hell had the teapot gone? But she gritted her teeth and took it from the pastor who had found it on the table behind the pile of books and greasy art magazines, carried it to the counter, dropped in a teabag and poured the not-yet-boiling water in. She could *feel* the assault of his grimace behind her. When she turned with the full pot, he leaped up, took it from her, and filled both teacups, not waiting for any semblance of steeping. Clearly, he was as eager as she was to get this – whatever it was – over with.

"Steven sent you." Steven probably made a fair-sized donation to the church.

"He's a good son; he's concerned about you." He glanced around the room and up at the cobwebs in the corners, where the dark-beamed ceiling met the crumbling once-white plaster walls, then over to the stove, and, without speaking, at the same moment as she realized that again she hadn't turned off the burner, he jumped up, in two strides was at the stove, cut the flame and was back at the table again, fixing on her once more, comically, that hyper-intense pale blue gaze of his.

"What a bore you are," she said, though pleasantly.

"He said you would be angry."

"He wants my property; he wants me to sign a power of attorney. How Christian is that?" The pastor's left cheek did a minute, quick dance; she could feel him wanting to draw back.

Good.

"He wants your well-being, as we all do," he responded, his voice soft, leaning closer to her, "although he did say you would say that, even that you believe that."

"Do you know what this place is worth? If not the house, at least this large lot in this truly refined and elegant area?" She could hear herself hissing. How she mourned the dead fruit trees in the small orchard at the back of the yard near where a fishpond had once been. Never mind. She didn't believe herself that this was all that Steven wanted, but it seemed easier to defend herself with this claim. "I'm told a couple of million." There, case closed. She managed to push her chair back an inch or two, enough that she could get herself to a standing position without falling or taking the hand he proffered.

"I don't like you," she told him. "I think it is *diabolical* of you to come here and try to *coerce* an old woman into doing something so *profound*, so *inalterable* that she does not want to do, purely for your own reasons." Her word choice delighted her, as mostly she couldn't think of words when she wanted them. She knew what they were but, slippery fish, they swam cunningly just beyond her grasp. "I will stay here; I will die here in my own house where I was..." she was about to say "born" but she hadn't been born here. But then, who would remember that? It was nearly a hundred years ago and she could say anything she damn well pleased. "Born!" she said. "Where I gave birth to my three children," also not true; "Where I was married," sort of true, and only with her second husband, the reception had been in the back garden when it was splendid with flowers; "Where my mother died," true; "and where I lived my whole life." Except for her years in art school in the east of the country, and the few she spent in New York, and the five or so when she had lived in Europe with her first husband, Piers. And then there were those years after a heart attack felled her second husband, Reuben, her children's father, when she had had to go out to schools across the country to teach and earn some money, her own practice as an artist not having made her a penny until lately – stuff she had done as a young woman mostly – when she no longer cared about money and didn't need it anyway. Except to pay the taxes on this monstrous abode of hers. She must not ever forget to pay the taxes.

"I want you to leave now." His expression didn't change; he simply stood as if he had been planning to all along, for a brief second rested one hand lightly on her shoulder, walked out of the room, and down the hall. She struggled to her feet again and followed him, bumping against the wall – she had a tendency these days to wander a bit to the right. When it wasn't to the left.

At the door, he said, "You phone me if you need anything. The church is here to help. And Steven and your daughters have your best interests at heart. They are not trying to steal from you or to mistreat you. They want you to be comfortable and safe in your last years." She wanted to slam the door while he was still standing in it, but it was too heavy and while she was wrestling with it, he had stepped out onto the wide verandah, about to go, then quickly turned back again. "A power of attorney –" but she managed to get the door shut on the rest of his sentence, then pulled back the filthy – even she recognized that the damn thing was filthy – sheer curtain that covered the narrow window beside the door with its bevelled and stained glass for which a collector had offered her a small fortune not so long ago, and watched Reverend Gower trot down the front steps, and then the straight-as-an-arrow path to the gate which he opened carefully, and shut with even more care, then went round his car, pausing at the driver's door to look up to the front of her house where she stood gazing out at him, then got in and drove away.

She hoped he had seen the finger.

She went back to the kitchen, the single room in which she now lived, to the darkest corner closest to the sofa that was now her bed, where, on the counter in plain view, except for the shadows, she kept her scotch. Somewhere there should be a glass. She found it in the sink, rinsed it vaguely, and, not bothering to dry it, poured in a good dollop, and sat on her sofa with it.

The next thing she knew her middle daughter Karen was standing in the kitchen, staring straight at her with an expression of mild horror while a second woman, a stranger in professional dress (navy jacket, white blouse, tailored tan slacks) stood beside Karen, gazing around with undisguised interest at Grace's arrangements.

"Who is she?" Grace demanded, although she knew perfectly well: social worker, probably the Mrs. Crowley on whom she had hung up at least three times and for whom she had twice refused to open the door. "Go away, both of you. Right now!" This tone had subdued her children, even as late as into their teens. When neither woman moved, she cast about for some other weapon in her sadly shrunken arsenal: don't answer the door, don't answer the phone, scream louder at people than they are screaming at you, cut them dead with your scintillating wit, recite your rights, then recite them again. She could see that she was moving toward the end of possibilities. She would not budge. She would not.

"Mother, where are your manners? Take Mrs. Crowley into the front room while I do a little tidy…while I make some tea."

"I loathe tea," Grace said. "Would you like a drink?" she asked Mrs. Crowley, but the scotch bottle seemed to have disappeared.

Mrs. Crowley bestirred herself. "I think it is time we had at least a conversation," she said. For once Grace didn't detect unctuousness, or the superciliousness that she had long ago discovered was the voice used mostly to address the old: the old as stubborn, offensive in their very existence, newly stupid, ineffective and always helpless, too close to death to be bothered with except as packages to be bathed and humped around in wheelchairs.

"At just what point did I stop being a human being?" she inquired.

Karen said quickly, "Mother! No one said…"

Grace had managed to get to her feet, Karen apparently not having noticed what she was trying to do and therefore not helping, and Mrs. Crowley watching her again with that expression of neutral interest, as if they were not two people standing a few feet apart in the same room, but that Grace was only a bloody – what was that? *hologram* – as if Grace was only an electronic projection of her former self.

"Have you been smoking again?" Karen asked, trying but failing to sound neutral as Mrs. Crowley seemed to do with such ease.

"I never stopped," Grace said. She was moving past the two women toward the door into the hall. She found that, although she was fuming, as she always did at being told what to do by people less than half her age, she was curious to see what her front parlour looked like these days. It had been months since she had last seen it. She felt as though she were visiting childhood friends, filled with curiosity to see what time had done to them, but hugely disappointed to discover they were still the same bloody people.

Somebody had covered the furniture with old sheets. She tried to throw off the one covering the brocade loveseat but lost her balance and would have fallen if Mrs. Crowley – "Please call me Toni" – hadn't caught her.

"Never mind. Let's just sit," Mrs. Crowley said. The woman

plunked herself down on the sheet-covered parlour chair across from Grace, set her overly-large purse on the rug, opened it and pulled out some sort of electronic gizmo – an electronic notebook, it would seem, as she began to write in it. Although Grace's hearing wasn't at all good, she could hear crashes and bangs coming from the kitchen and the clashing and ding of pots. This meant that Karen was furious at the mess and was letting her know.

"She wants me to move immediately into a nursing home… a…an assisted living place, whatever that is."

Mrs. Crowley said, "I expect you know perfectly well what that is." She smiled at Grace as if her tactics were amusing. "I deal exclusively with the old and while all the usual applies, I find it kind of fun to watch you all use the same dodges when it suits you: I'm old, you can't expect me to know that; I'm old, you do it" – here she switched tones – "Just because I'm old doesn't mean I can't look after myself."

In spite of herself, Grace laughed. "Well, you can hardly blame us," she said. "We have so few options left."

"You still have your brain."

"Of course, I do, although my children think I'm far gone into senility."

"Children often confuse perceptual difficulties and the new slowness of mental organization for a damaged brain."

"Also, any sense one maintains of one's right to autonomy." Grace huffed this out furiously.

"They do want you to move, and I am pretty convinced, now that I've met all three of them, that they really do have your welfare at heart. They really do not believe you to be capable any longer of taking care of yourself. They are truly afraid for you."

"I notice you didn't say, 'They love you.'"

"Don't you believe they do?"

"Actually, no. They used to, but that dwindled and died as the years of my recalcitrance extended themselves until you find me as I am now. Just a bloody, old nuisance. And they are bound by now-worthless family ties to keep an eye on me. This does not include caring about what I want."

"That's a harsh judgement on your own children."

"They cannot even begin to imagine themselves old," Grace said, and heard the querulousness in her own voice, heard even the edge of despair, which served only to further infuriate her.

"They believe that when their time comes they will manage things much better," Mrs. Crowley suggested. "That they will never find themselves in this position."

"What, you mean alive? And with a will? When she gets finished in there I won't be able to find a damn thing," she said, gesturing toward the kitchen. "I need a cigarette."

"And that's another thing. They think you will burn the house down with yourself in it."

"And still I want a cigarette." Grace fumbled around in the pocket of the apron she seemed, inexplicably, to be wearing, and lo and behold, found a squashed pack of cigarettes and a small box of matches. It was like magic, and she held them up to show Mrs. Crowley, who leaned forward to help her light a match and held it to the end of the cigarette as Grace puffed on it.

"You want me to agree to leave."

"In lieu of that, to agree to a home-care worker coming in each day to make sure you are safe and have had a hot meal. Or Meals on Wheels could come every day. Maybe that would be better. But first and foremost, why do you refuse to move to a safer, warmer, more comfortable place?"

"I can't believe you are even asking me that question. I was born here and have lived here almost all my life." Her cigarette seemed to have gone out, in fact, had disappeared, but there was a scattering of ash on her apron's lap.

"No," Mrs. Crowley said. "That's a fiction, although you have lived here many, many years, even when you were a child. But frankly, between you and me, I don't quite believe that's what the obsessiveness is all about."

Grace studied her carefully. "I had certainly never imagined that you might be interesting."

"Are you afraid of dying?"

"Of course, but then, also, not a bit."

"I mean, are you afraid that if you move, you'll die."

"There's no question about that."

"Is it – I think I'm getting it – is it just that old question of making your own decisions about your own life?"

"Wow!" Grace said. "I bet you went to graduate school." There was a silence. A thin stream of smoke from a newly-materialized ashtray curled upward beside Mrs. Crowley's elbow. Hmm. So that's what had happened to her cigarette. She considered lighting a second one, just to show that she could, but it seemed too much trouble. "And also, they want me – Steven especially – to sign a power of attorney document. So he can sell this place out from under me and force me into moving."

"He will have to go to court to get that from you if you refuse to give it," Mrs. Crowley said. She sighed. "He needs lawyers and doctors to certify your inability to look after yourself ..." She let her voice trail away. "He will do it, you know. I suspect the very fact of your extreme age will guarantee his success. He has been holding off in hope that you will consent on your own to a move and a sale."

Grace said, "I wish for a drink. I need a drink."

"Not wise, under the circumstances," Mrs. Crowley said.

"I hurt all over," Grace said, that querulous note returning to her voice. But it was true.

"They'll give me strong drugs for the aches and pains, but I can't have a goddamn drink? What's the matter with them? Do they think my heart might stop?" She had been yelling. She knew this because there was Karen standing in the door, carrying a tray with the teapot and teacups on it.

"Mom," she said. "Please."

"It's all right, Karen," the social worker said. "We are doing fine."

Grace wanted to tell them both to get out right now, but her mouth was suddenly parched for tea, so she held back the stream of invective she had been hoarding.

"There is also the route of getting the house condemned," Mrs. Crowley was saying. "City inspectors and all that." But just as her daughter set down the tray on the small table between them, Grace realized her apron was on fire, and already the social worker was pushing past Karen, nearly knocking her over, and had grabbed at the apron, tearing it off Grace, rolling it into a ball and stomping on it.

"You see!" Karen shouted. "Mother? Do you see?"

Having tidied the parlour, taken away the tea things, and seen her settled with a small salad and a chicken sandwich on white bread at her kitchen table from which Karen had cleared away the mayonnaise jar, the ketchup bottle, the jar of mouldy raisin chutney, the raspberry jam and saucer of honey, the leftover bread crusts from a day or two before, the stack of old magazines, and whatever else had been sitting there within handy reach, the visitors prepared to leave. "Susan will come by in the morning on her way to work," Karen said. "She'll get you a hot breakfast. By the way, the grocer left your box of supplies on the verandah. I brought it in and put the things away. And…" Grace's heart sped up, pattering away lightly low in her throat. "And Mrs. Crowley and I are getting in a home-care worker to give you a bath." She held up a hand shoulder-high, palm first. "Mother, you smell of urine. A bath and clean clothes."

"Just how do you propose I get upstairs to the bathroom?" Grace asked. She used the toilet off the kitchen and, as far as she could remember, bathed in the kitchen sink.

"She will bathe you down here in the kitchen where it is warm. I've brought some clean clothes for you." Not waiting for her to wind herself up to rage again, her daughter and the social worker said a cheery, "See you soon," and were gone.

She was amazed to find herself hungry, the sandwich was delicious and she savoured every bite, although it was, of course, too much food for her. Then she lay down on the sofa wedged into the corner of the room and on which, years before, the family dog and occasional cat usually slept. There, she fell asleep.

She must have been dreaming, because a voice had been shouting in her ear, "Watch out! Pay attention!" She opened her eyes and saw that the room had darkened; it was twilight, she must have slept all afternoon. On a previous visit, Karen or Susan or possibly even Steven had moved a standing lamp to the end of the couch where she placed her head and now, sitting up, she clicked it on and studied the room in which she found herself. Still the kitchen, no flame burning on the stove, no smoke rising from anywhere that she could see, no tap gushing water, and on the table only one pretty little mouse chewing away at the remains of her sandwich. She could see Reuben sitting across the room from her, in the shadows in the corner where there remained an old wooden kitchen chair that she had once used to stand on when she needed to reach things high in the cupboard. She couldn't quite make out his face, but it was her second husband all right, wearing his baggy, dirt-smudged, denim pants, that he used when he gardened and his faded plaid flannel shirt over a worn-out blue dress shirt. She had always liked him best in that outfit for some reason. So masculine, so earthy, or something.

"What do you want?" she inquired, as if she were annoyed by

his constant neediness.

"The rhododendrons need cutting," he said. "And somebody should fertilize the rose bushes."

"Those bushes are dead," she said, and then, maybe a trifle plaintively, "aren't they?" The chair creaked as he stood. Now she could see his face; how lined it was, how cheerful his expression. "My girl," he said, tenderly. They both laughed. Then he was gone.

Once she had seen a bird that way: some bird she didn't recognize, in fact doubted even existed so strange it was, and when she glanced down for an instant to see where her feet were, the bird had vanished, just as Reuben had vanished, but both had left behind the same absence. Not as when things just weren't where you thought they were – your car keys, your glass of gin, your hairbrush – but when the absence itself becomes a thing. Very well, the bird, the man, both had come from another reality and when they had gone back to it, the space between the two realities didn't close right away. You could still see it. How wonderful that was. What unexpected, vast hope that gave her.

But, oh dear, Grace thought. Something is definitely up. A voice inside her head said, *They will now turn off your gas and electricity and your water. They will say it is because your house is unsafe. They will take you out when the wrecking crew arrives.* There was no bloody way she was leaving until they hauled her out as the house came down around her. At this, it occurred to her that her mother, exquisitely brought up as she was, would be angry with her for making a spectacle of herself. For giving up her dignity.

Steven, she knew it, would be along soon, probably as soon as she was bathed and in clean clothes. He would bring that lawyer again; he would bring documents for her to sign and if she refused, and they all knew she would, he would return with the lawyer again and two medical doctors and they would take everything away from her.

"I am clinging to my very soul right now," she cried, raising a fist and looking up to the dingy ceiling where cobwebs hung down and dead flies stuck to years-old flypaper turned in the golden light from the lamp. How beautiful they were, transparent columns of light, her ceiling a glinting, shimmering, speckled garden. "I am clinging to my very soul." Whispered, this time. "Mother," Steven had said patiently to her. "You cannot fall again; your bones are too fragile; if you fall again, you will…"

"You bring death with you," she said. He had begun to cry. I have come to this, she thought, I have made my children cry; I have made my *son* cry.

It was very dark outside now, probably past midnight, and the dawn would bring her end.

That was what Reuben's visit was all about; it was to tell her she had reached the end of choice. She could feel her heart squeezing and releasing in her chest. Was it her imagination, or was it weaker and slower than usual? Well, why not? she asked herself. I'll soon be one hundred years. By using the chair on one side of her knees and the thin wooden column of the lamp on the other, she managed to stand. The back of her skirt felt warm and she recognized that she had wet herself. She would not allow herself to think *again*.

She was so very stiff from lying down all the afternoon, but by pulling herself along from piece of furniture to piece of furniture, she made it to the sink, which she grasped and held onto, thinking she would perhaps boil the kettle again and make herself a nice, hot cup of tea. But Reuben had returned, not that she could see him, but she could feel him around her, warm and loving as he had usually been, or was at his best. Scrabbling about on the counter she found the stack of magazines that Karen must have forgotten to take with her. She pulled the stack toward her, fumbled in her pocket, and when she found what she wanted, knocked the magazine on top of the pile over toward the sink. It fell half in and half out, spreading its pages awkwardly. She pulled two pages off, the ones that had refused to lie down neatly, and with her other hand, opened her package of matches and extracted one. This, she saw at once, would fail; she would only fall down or do some other such stupid thing of the kind she had found herself doing over and over again the last few months. Or was it years?

But somehow or other the burner was on, the blue and yellow flames warming her and lighting up even the dark corner where previously Reuben had sat. She sighed, gazing into the darkness out the window one more time, although she could see only the wrinkled visage of a very old woman, and then put the magazine's pages to the fire. When they caught and flamed high in her hand, she managed to reach up and over to the grimy curtains that framed the window, pushed the flame toward them, and waited. In a moment, the cheery red and orange flames had chased each other up the cloth and now, the bent and stained ceiling panels were beginning to smoke.

Satisfied, she found the bottle of scotch – how had it gotten there? – poured herself a drink, and sat down on her sofa to savour it while black smoke began to roll down from the ceiling and the fire grew, all the while, noisier and noisier, whistling and crackling and whooshing in a satisfying way.

ELEPHANTS

Inspired by Ernest Hemingway's "Hills Like White Elephants", 1927

SHE HAD BECOME AWARE OF A HIGH-PITCHED WHISTLE, STARTLING HER out of her reverie. It was the gallery's alarm; she must have been standing too close to the painting. All of them were familiar to her in reproduction but here, in real life at the Vancouver Art Gallery, the Emily Carrs were even more stunning in their richness and their brilliant simplicity; so direct, yet the pictures' – 'stories' – nearly swamped with a vast mystery, one, she thought, unknowable to us settlers. Maybe unknowable to First Nations people too, although like all of us poor benighted souls, they also think they've got life and death figured out. Although all roads lead to Rome, Dick the Anglican liked to say. How wonderful if the First Nations people were right, and truth lay in nature, in the earth. But she lived in a high-rise in the city now; it had been a couple of years since her feet had touched grass; what they (the First Nations) thought was truth was, sadly, nothing much to her any more.

She moved to the next painting – lots of totem poles in this one. She let her eyes move down first one, then the next one, and the next, studying the carved figures: ravens, bears, killer whales, even eagles, all the most striking creatures of the west coast realm. In a burst of playfulness, she tried to imagine giraffes, tigers, rhinoceroses carved on such poles, but couldn't think how such bulky and odd-shaped animals could be made to fit into so firmly, even ritually a defined space. Or hippopotamuses, or elephants. All of which brought her once again to the elephant still, after more than sixty years, in her possession.

The truth was, ever since her husband, Dick, had died two years earlier, she had not been able to stop thinking about Robert Thorley. Like a silly girl, she still thought sometimes of how beautiful his profile was, like an Apollo on an ancient Greek coin, although he wasn't Greek at all, but a hard-drinking American ex-serviceman, and a blond who was a dozen years older than her. Even though they only went out a few times before he simply disappeared from her life, the cheap little brass elephant he had given her on their first date had stayed, its red and green paint long since chipped off or worn away. (And by the way, she thought indignantly, if distantly so, why do we always turn to that epithet 'silly' about girls and never about boys who at that age were every bit as silly? Because of the way we girls were taught to be; being silly was feminine; *when I was a girl nobody expected better of us; silliness was* cute *in a girl*.)

Dick, to whom she had been married nearly sixty years, died thinking the brass elephant had come from her best girlfriend, Gwen, dead at fifty, in a car accident, possibly a suicide, but no one would ever know for sure. Not that Dick had even noticed the little brass animal in years even though, for some reason she couldn't explain herself – was it for Gwen? – she kept it in a prominent place on her dresser in the bedroom, lifting it to dust, and even now and then grasping it by its tiny upraised trunk to polish it. *The fact was – the fact is – that I lost my virginity to Robert Thorley.* Not hard to understand, in these days of ready pop psychology, why she had lied to Dick about where the trinket had come from. To tell the truth (hah!), she had never told him about Robert at all, Dick being naïve enough to believe she was a virgin when she said she was. Or had he only pretended to believe her? She had never been sure, and couldn't bring herself to ask. *Better to let sleeping dogs – or elephants – lie*, she told herself whenever, thinking of Gwen, rarely of Robert Thorley, she looked seriously at the elephant.

Was it wrong that she'd never told Dick the truth? Probably, she thought comfortably, but quickly knew that she wasn't sure about it being wrong. Maybe it wasn't, given the male ego, and all that. She wondered, as she often did, what Dick had lied about to her. Lots of things, she was willing to bet. Even though he was, as far as she knew, a good man. And who knew him better than she did?

An art major who had stopped painting years ago, Margaret had wanted to examine Carr's brushwork, but in this new world in which Dick had abandoned her, she should have known that everything was alarmed. Indignantly, she turned her back to the tiny white church in the monstrous green-shaded forest, and realized that the security guard, a stout woman with a grim expression wearing an official blue uniform, was standing right behind her. Had she been talking to herself? She closed her face, tilted her chin upward.

"How does one see the brushwork?" she asked, not looking at the guard.

"Video, ma'am," the guard said, pointing to the doorway on her left at the end of the gallery.

"Ahh," she replied, as if grateful. Then, "Excuse me," passing the unlovely woman as if *she* were being the nuisance, and not her, Margaret, once known to all as Maggie, and to Robert – what a thing to think of now – as *Maggie Breakheart*. She couldn't help but laugh. If only she had a living friend left with whom she could move through the gallery so if she laughed no one would think of her as a crazy old lady, but they were all gone now, starting with once-pretty, tormented Gwen and the car accident that probably wasn't an accident – the older Margaret grew the more sure she became that it was no accident – and ending with dear Myra only two weeks ago. Hardly unexpected at her age, but still, Myra had been well enough to buy a plane ticket to Vancouver to come with her to see (*before we die, ha ha*) this marvelous Emily Carr show. And if all went well, they had thought of going in the New Year, perhaps (always with the crossed fingers that one of them wouldn't be incapacitated if not dead) to Toronto to the Mary Pratt show. Damn it! And then Myra goes and dies. Eighty-two or not, she was inconsiderate as hell. She searched in her handbag for a tissue and blew her nose. Did she want to look at the video of Carr's brushwork? She thought not, having always believed that too much examination earned small rewards, and had a stronger tendency to destroy what truly mattered, and anyway, she had only asked the question so the guard would know she was a knowledgeable art lover and not merely a daft old lady.

It was lunchtime, and she had no one to eat with. Never mind, it was an art gallery with its own café, and one used to single older women, where she wouldn't be ignored, made to wait unnecessarily, treated as if she were merely an annoyance and not a real customer like everybody else. *Getting old is such a bugger*, and because Dick was dead and couldn't criticize her, she muttered the word out loud. "Bugger!"

"I beg your pardon?" asked the sweet little girl serving her at the cafeteria, her black tie a touch askew against her thin white shirt. For once she had got a solicitous one. *Well brought up; maybe even loves her grandmother*, and when Margaret failed to reply, not sure what the little thing was referring to, she asked, "Would you like some wine with that?"

"White," Margaret said, as if this had been her plan all along. Bad enough to be alone in a hotel room in Vancouver with Myra dead, and having to see the paintings that they had made plans for so long to see together by herself. Their last great adventure, although, of course, there was still Mary Pratt. She'd soon be dead herself; might as well have a glass of wine even though wine did nasty things to her digestion and she would then regret even this tiny amount.

Ahead of her in the cafeteria line was a couple even more elderly than she, the two of them shorter also; almost indistinguishable one from the other. Each had a tray, each putting identical things on it: small green salad, some meat or fish in cream with mushroom caps rising out of the mix, a scoop of rice, a custard dessert. No wine. Gwen had always drunk too much. Ever since she came back from Europe, how long ago now? Sixty years ago at least. Always giggly or more at parties, and then that stupid marriage to Bright – Jim Bright. Handsome, not bright, in fact, a bit stupid even if more or less successful. Big brick house. And domineering.

But the men were all domineering in those days, and women mostly just accepted it, except for Gwen, whose answer to Bright's dictatorial ways had been increasingly just to get drunk, a response that, to tell the truth and even knowing full well this wasn't a good thing, Margaret had always rather admired. Until he put her into that hospital and told everybody it was to dry her out. Poor Gwen. He was not a nice man, although Margaret thought he loved her. Something, anyway. He felt something for her. If she could now, after so many years of living, say one thing about being alive, it was that *it is all a mystery to me. It is all mystery.*

The couple who had been ahead of her, who had taken a long time picking out cutlery and condiments as if world peace hinged on each choice, then filling glasses with water, were now sitting down in the same row where she had planned to sit. The small tables were crowded too closely together; she picked the last table on her right in order to leave a couple of empty tables between her and them, and also to give herself a bit more room. She watched them surreptitiously, leaning back in her chair and pretending to glance around the room, or down at the map of the galleries she had set beside her plate. They were tweedy, rumpled, shapeless, and both wore crumpled, pudding-like, no-colour cloth hats on their heads.

Probably English, she thought, maybe over from Victoria for the day, also here to see the wonderful work by Emily Carr: a woman who had never married, had almost no success in her life as a painter, by all accounts not much liked by others, and in old age became strange (wasn't there something about a monkey?) a baglady type before there were bag ladies. And yet, the paintings! *What the world does to people of talent, while the hucksters prosper.* She wanted to say this very loudly but by pressing her lips together, managed not to. Just as well, a clutch of young women in their tight, bright dresses, giant handbags tucked under their upper arms, were setting down their loaded trays and seating themselves noisily around the table immediately across the narrow aisle from her. She put on her elderly-woman blinkers, knowing she could be nothing but ridiculous to them.

The elderly couple who had attracted her interest, she noticed, did not look at her, didn't glance around, not even once, nor up from their plates, in fact, not even to look at each other. As she watched them while pretending not to, she knew for a fact that they had not spoken to each other all day, maybe not even for days, and, for the first time since Dick's death, a tide of relief swept over her at this perception, that his dying had at least spared her this humiliation. This thought was so shocking and unexpected, and so profound that she didn't doubt it: the couple did not speak to each other any more; they existed in mutual silence thinking their own thoughts and no longer bothering at all to communicate them: Out of hopelessness? Out of a sense that they had emotionally, as a couple, gone everywhere they knew how to go and had no interest any more in trying to go further, or elsewhere? A mutual life, or life as a mutual endeavor had ended; and they had given up, and moved now together strictly as an automaton.

Her thoughts went back to poor Gwen, and it occurred to her that perhaps Jim Bright was not such an awful man, but only that

Gwen saw this too in her future with him, and could not bear it. And here she was, Maggie Breakheart, glad that Dick, whom she had loved, and missed now as if she had lost a part of each of her cells, had died before they had reached this point. Both she and Gwen had glimpsed something else once, when they were young, whatever that thing was, and Gwen couldn't ever let it go, while Maggie, for some reason she didn't understand in herself but thought might be a failing, could, and had, and never once acknowledged she had done so, not even to herself.

For the first time that she could recall, it occurred to her that elephants were famous for their memory.

Jim Bright had had Gwen committed even though he loved her. He had thought himself as the most fortunate man on earth when she had agreed to marry him, but he was ashamed in front of their friends to acknowledge that the most beautiful girl on earth had, in his care, turned into a drunk, and, worse, one who turned out not to be able to have children. He had her committed because he was so angry with her, because he had come to hate her. Of course Gwen had plowed into that concrete abutment on purpose; it was no accident. Margaret and Gwen, the two prettiest girls in class, and Gwen advising her to drop the gorgeous Robert – *He is much too old for you, and besides, you know you can't trust a man who is that good looking* – sage advice, as if Gwen were a hundred and ten instead of maybe nineteen. And yet, even at that, she had been right, if only for Maggie and not for herself.

And her mother, as they worked together changing the sheets on her brothers' beds, said to her out of the blue, in a low voice Maggie didn't recognize, didn't think she had ever heard before from her, "He will never marry you." Startled, Maggie had looked down the length of the white to her mother who stood loosely holding each corner of the sheet in her fingers, as if she had forgotten what she was doing, her face turned away, her expression one Maggie wasn't sure about, but thought might be grief. Maggie had not replied. She knew even then, even at nineteen or so, that what her mother said was true. They began to tuck the sheet in under the mattress, muttering to each other, "That corner's crooked," and, "Give me another inch here, would you?" politely. The war barely over, and Robert gone before she had had anywhere near enough of him.

And then the mourning. Good Lord, what an idiot girl she'd been.

And here I am in the Vancouver Art Gallery looking at the Emily Carrs and eating lunch alone, I who was once called by a devilishly handsome man, "Maggie Breakheart". What did I call him? Robert, Bob, Bobbie? No, Rob; I called him Rob. And just like that she was back in his arms, his mouth was on hers. Hurriedly she lifted her wine to her lips and drank a too-large gulp, its chill hitting the roof of her mouth and then icing her throat, freezing out the memory. Not that she desired sex – here she felt like standing up and announcing this to the table of four young women on her other side, all engrossed in their conversation, heads together, out of which floated the words which, it seemed to Maggie she saw, rather than heard: "Jamie," and "Trev," and "Ryan."

Not sex, that is not what one wants when one is past eighty! She was indignant – *it must be the wine* – that anyone would think that. One needed to move on and one didn't actually know how to do that. *Oh, dear. Had she ever moved on from Robert Thorley?* Moved on to what? She wondered if the old couple down the row of tables from her had figured things out and had moved on. Was that the best reason as to why they never even bothered to speak to one another?

She examined that visceral second when she had felt the heat of Robert's mouth on hers: What had she really felt when she found herself so abruptly immersed in it? Impatience.

Annoyance. Yes, the memory of what it had been like to be in love – no, *in heat* – with a man. She frowned into her salmon salad. How trivial it seemed now: How one swooned and yearned and magnified every emotion, every sensation, desiring, *willing* one's self to be lost in it, to be carried away, believing that this was the meaning of life, that this was at last the fulfilled promise of her otherwise wasted, meaningless existence. The sheer absurdity, the wrongheadedness of this notion stunned her so that she lifted her head, looked down the table at the old couple who were now spooning in their custards – perhaps they were not that old after all – still not looking at each other, nor speaking, and then to the four girls on her right. And Gwen, poor Gwen, lost forever.

The young women, all ordinary-looking, nothing special about any of them, no Maggie Breakhearts or poor lovely Gwens there, were still laughing together, as if their world was the only one that mattered, indeed, the only one that had ever mattered. *How life would sober them.* But even as she thought this both sad and wonderful idea, a cloud that was neither vapour, visible and palpable, nor emotion, was moving around her. It was, in fact, more as if it had always been there, but it seemed, nonetheless, to be coming from the four ordinary young women, wafting across the short distance between their table and hers; it was as if, only now, for the first time in her life, she perceived what was always there, and always had been.

If she had been standing, she would have fallen to her knees so powerful and all-encompassing was it, yet soft and exquisitely delicate, too wonderful, too honest to be merely alluring: It was, her breath held as it dawned on her, the *essence* of their beauty; it was the ageless, always divine, beauty of the Feminine. No wonder that for this ideal men would rise up, even off their deathbeds!

How life is illuminated for you, when you are old.

She felt a distant urge to cry, mixed in with an equally distant joy; her body was flushing with the wonder of it, her heart light as a feather rising in the still air, her now-heavy body that feather. *If you wait long enough, if you think hard, but not too hard; if you hold yourself still* – but she sounded like one of those sappy television gurus who make their millions fooling, mostly, women.

But she had seen what she had seen. Those poor girls, thinking their nail polish and seductive glances, half-denied even as they gave them, their too-high heels that crippled them, the low necklines and short skirts, the carefully tended, shining hair, would earn them worlds to rule. Her mind raced to all the raped women, all the brutalized, the murdered women, to all those enslaved women around the world and through the ages – men so terrified of women's power they sought to stamp it out – terrified of this *thing* that was surely divine in its origin. What to make of this?

What had it to do with Gwen and with herself and Robert Thorley, and Jim Bright, and Dick?

She realized, now, that over the years in some peculiar way she didn't quite understand, she had begun to think of that small despoiled, yet apparently indestructible brass elephant as having been Gwen's. But that it was not Gwen's, but Robert Thorley's careless yet calculated gift seemed to her to be the lie; in her heart it was a gift from Gwen and always had been, a remembrance of her and the pain of what it truly is to be a silly girl.

SOOTHSAYER

Inspired by Edgar Allan Poe's poem, "The Raven", 1845

THE OTHER DAY, AS I WAS SITTING READING IN THE LIVING ROOM OF MY condo, I became aware of banging, thumping and scrabbling noises going on somewhere outside. I have mild age-related hearing loss, which makes it hard for me to locate sound, so I listened for a moment in perplexity. I realized, finally, that the noise was coming from the roof immediately above me. Because I live on the third and top floor of my building, and there is no attic between me and the roof, whatever goes on up there interests me. I decided I wasn't hearing boots – somebody replacing shingles, or checking air conditioners – and I couldn't imagine how small children could get up there, or the large wild rabbits which populate the underbrush all over the neighbourhood. I put down my book, struggled out of my armchair, went to my balcony door, and opened it a foot or so without stepping outside. It was fall and cold and I wasn't wearing a jacket or sweater.

My kitchen extends along my balcony at right angles to the living room and the open door in which I stood. There, on the edge of that extended section of roof, stood the biggest raven I've ever seen. It was facing toward the roof, so I could see only one of its legs; it was moving in that jittery fashion of birds, and, hanging loosely from its shiny, grey-black beak was the jointed leg and part of the haunch of an equally large bird. The raven had been looking at me with one eye, but then it bent its head and scratched awkwardly about, it seemed to me, to secure its grip on its burden. I saw then that below the raven on the balcony floor was a pool of dark blood sizeable enough that it was hard to imagine it had come from a mere bird and not from a larger animal. I was so shocked both by the grotesqueness of the spectacle and by the very size of the raven, and thinking that another bird had torn off its leg – that it was holding its own leg in his beak – that my heart began to beat faster, and, wanting only to escape the ghastly scene, I pulled the door shut. Almost at once though, my conscience overcame me and I opened the door a slit, thinking of finding a way to help the raven. But it was far too big for me to hold onto, and even if I managed to trap it, I realized, I wouldn't know what to do next. The noise still going on over my head, although less frantically now, I pulled the door shut once more, rushed to my laptop and googled 'animal rescue'.

I was surprised to find a number almost at once, but before I dialed it I thought I had better check on the bird one more time. There it was, the leg now secured in its beak, with those giant claws, the spread of each easily the size of one of my hands, perched in almost the same place, still facing toward the expanse of roof (as I looked out over the city) but about five feet to my right and above me, and its one large – in the clear light – buff-coloured eye that I could see, staring right at me. I saw at once that the leg in the bird's beak wasn't its own. Behind the raven, well out of range of what I could see from against the wall, were other birds whose running and sporadic thuds I continued to hear.

The raven stared at me with its one round eye, and I stared back, hoping for, I think, some kind of message from it, some sign of – could it be *humanity?* – in its gaze, but I saw nothing, just that flat beige-tan circle, and maybe a tiny dark dot in its middle. Its gaze was unflinching and the very blankness of its stare combined with its relentlessness chilled and alarmed me. In a sudden rush of fear that the raven might attack me, and as I had seen that it was intact and not in need of help, I shut the door and locked it, and hours passed before I looked out again. All was quiet by then, and the raven was gone.

Unlike most old women who complain that they haven't a man of any type left in their lives, and all they see now that they are old is other old women, I have been left only with men. The first is my son Herald who, since I have fulfilled my role by giving birth to him and raising him to late adolescence, though he loved me once, now cares nothing for me, and who has busied himself year by year with wiping me out of his world. Herald has never married. Other than me, there have been no women in his life, so he has given me no grandchildren, and is the only one left of my family. He is an anthropologist and sometimes a comparative religionist and teaches at a university in Montreal, although he is close to retirement (I still think of him as about thirty) and after he does retire, will probably stay home and write books, which is more or less what he is doing now. Once in a while, on his trips across the country to this university or that, he stops off for a short visit with me. Otherwise, I no longer see him, and have succeeded, after years of trying, to move him from the forefront of my mind to somewhere much further back, so that his absence from my life long ago stopped causing me such suffering.

The other is my friend, Alex Sealy, whom I have also not seen in a couple of years, although we continue to talk on the phone now and then. A couple of weeks after the raven incident, my phone rang, which it seldom does any more, and it was Alex's oldest son calling to tell me that Alex had *passed away*. I grew angry, wanting to interrupt and say, "died," but managed to refrain. It was all I could do to remain polite and properly grateful that he had taken the time to call me and also, to give me the time and place of Alex's interment, which of course, as it's taking place in Toronto and I am in Calgary, I won't attend.

"In case you are ever in the city and want to visit his..." Here I lost track: he used some term that meant the place where the urn containing his ashes would be placed. Is it a columbarium? Or is that a medical test? Such an unwieldly term, a holdover from the Latin, I suppose. I hung up quickly, not even bothering to write down the information the son, Josh I think, had just given me. I said to the now dead phone, "I would have come for a proper funeral." But that was probably not true either. The uneasiness I hadn't been able to shake since what I had taken to calling 'the raven incident,' stemmed from my knowledge that, in all cultures I know of, the raven is a bird of prophecy.

Alex had been a friend of my husband's with whom I'd once had a flirtation. It was nothing more than that, but we were attracted to one another to such a degree that we both went out of our way to hide it whenever my husband, Ed, was around. When Alex finally married Elizabeth, a girl I'd barely known, Ed and I didn't go to his wedding although we had planned to, because Ed had a nasty flu, and Herald, just a baby, was running a fever, and I was too worried about him to go away overnight. Shortly afterward, Alex and a pregnant Elizabeth moved away to Toronto, too far for us to travel to without a very good reason.

Years passed, as they have a tendency to do, and Alex had been married maybe a dozen years, Ed and I closer to twenty. I was in Winnipeg at a nursing conference – I am an emergency room nurse-manager, or used to be, and was there to deliver a paper on stream-lining services – and, as I walked down the hall of the hotel where we were all staying, a door ahead of me opened, and out came Alex. As if there was something magical about our meeting, that is, it felt predestined (we told each other in a mutual attempt at exoneration) or more simply, why fight it; *it was meant to be.*

He was there on business too, though not medical; he was an engineer, and he was also alone. What can I say? It was such a long time ago and we were, if not exactly young, still in the prime of life, Ed had become the original fuddy-duddy, as we used to say, and Alex and I were as attracted to one another as we had ever been. I am not quite ashamed to say that we had dinner and then spent the night together in his room. The next morning he left for home as did I. A few years later Ed died, and I moved into an apartment and then, a couple of years after that, having finally accepted that Ed wouldn't be coming back, into this condo.

Eventually Alex called to find out how I was doing without Ed and to tell me that he and Elizabeth had split up, that the kids were grown and gone, and she had gone back to Medicine Hat to live. (I remember looking up the name, Medicine Hat, to find it probably refers to the head-covering of an aboriginal shaman. Herald may have succeeded in extracting himself from me, but as time passes, I seem to absorb more of him.) Alex had moved into a bachelor condo in downtown Toronto, and had no intentions of ever marrying again.

Another two or three years passed, during which we spoke only rarely, and then, one day, Alex phoned me.

"I've had enough of the fast life in downtown Toronto," he said, not laughing. "I want to be able to go hiking in the mountains; I want to have trees around me, to see the occasional bear or elk or moose." I wanted to tell him that for these things downtown Calgary wasn't much better than downtown Toronto, but this turned out to be unnecessary: he found an acreage west and south of town, not too far out, and moved there. By this time, I was sixty-seven and he was seventy and the fact of our ages was finally beginning to sink in. We saw each other now and then, and although our relationship was erotic, it was more pleasant than passionate, as it had been in our youth.

He was adamant though: we would not be moving in together, much less getting married, which annoyed me mightily, first, because of *his* apparent assumption that *I* was assuming we would get married and second, because – I suspect I had harboured some hopes – he had just informed me that we wouldn't be. Now I think he was right about each of us continuing to live on our own. As a consequence, I got busy with my friends and my volunteer activities, which began to take up most of my time, and traveled with my girlfriends – "the old babes," as Alex used to call them until I pointed out that they were younger than he was, which quite took him aback, although in the end, he said, "I guess they are!" and seemed, with this realization, to undergo a bit of a spiritual re-thinking, although of what exactly it consisted, I don't know.

After a while, as one or the other of my women friends got sick in ways that would only get worse, so that our holidays dwindled and ceased, and as Alex was still out there on the acreage, building bird houses and keeping bees and what-not, I began to think: why should the life of an old person be a poor copy of the life of a young one? As if to be an old person was merely to be a failed young one. And then I began to wonder what the life of an old person could be on its own, as if there had never been a young person, with her ceaseless activity, her endless drama from excessive weeping to equally excessive excitement, inside this wrinkled and shapeless exterior. I asked Alex on one of his increasingly infrequent visits.

"Interesting thought," he said. "Let's see. If I were born the way I am now; if there were no young people in the world, only aged ones with their debilities and incapacities...."

"They wouldn't be debilities and incapacities," we both said at once. "They'd be normal," I added. "We'd have to establish a whole new set of…I don't know…purposes?"

He said, "What are your purposes when you're young? Mostly just to be happy," answering himself. "But to be happy when you're young means finding a partner, getting an education, and then a job, being successful, and so on."

"Only the happy one still applies in old age," I said.

"Happy? No, I don't think so."

"What are you talking about?" I said. "Define happy."

"Let's not be ridiculous," he said. I bristled.

"Patriarchal scum."

"Bitch, crone, hag," he said to me. We could carry on in this manner for a good five minutes, and often had, but this time we agreed to both shut up and eat our dinners before they got cold. He had once told me in all seriousness that I was becoming a witch – "in the old-fashioned sense," he hastened to point out. I inquired as to his meaning.

"Someone who can see into the future and make prophecies," he told me. "Someone who can see the spirit world before she joins it."

I laughed at him and changed the subject although even then I could feel it coming true. But it doesn't do to have such a reputation. They don't burn you at the stake anymore; they just lock you up in an asylum, or else they drug you so heavily you might as well be locked up. Or dead.

I used to have friends who called themselves witches and who met in covens where they stood around in circles chanting and lighting candles and waving around sticks of incense. They were alert enough to know that I have some natural facility for the spirit world that they were always going on about, but whenever they asked me to join them, I laughed at them, always being careful to deny that I had any such abilities.

"Calgary is a terrible city for witchcraft," I used to tell them. "It's too commercialized and money-loving. Go to Victoria. I hear there are lots of your kind there." I had a friend who told me she had moved away from Victoria for that very reason, because random witches floating around the city had picked up on her vibes as a 'sensitive' and kept knocking on her door – perfect strangers, she told me – and asking her to join them, and she had gotten very sick of the whole business and moved to Kelowna. She claimed never to have been a practitioner, and died some years ago under myste-rious circumstances. It could have been suicide for all I know, but might have been something else. Witches are a jealous lot, and what they can do at a long distance you would not believe.

Later, as Alex and I were lounging on the sofa in front of my fake fireplace – fake because no wood, coal or ashes are involved – he said, "Of course, that could never happen because where would the babies come from?"

"If we didn't have happy, what would we have?"

"What we have now: hanging around waiting for the axe to fall."

"Honestly," I said. "For a smart man you say dumb things."

"Nobody can solve this problem," he said, in something that I might have called an anguished tone. "When you can't make babies, and you can't work, and you're not interested in curling, bowling, skydiving, travelling, or scrapbooking, what the hell are you going to do?"

"Read," I said. "Study. Think. Walk in nature."

"Well, that's original."

What could I do but sigh, because, of course, he was right. "There are things that it is impossible to learn when you are young, no matter how much you read and study." I could feel him turning his head to look at me; he was still a handsome man, even at eighty. But, I thought, so what?

"I'll give you that," he said at last, and we both sat staring into the gas-fueled fire.

That night may have been the last time he stayed over, but of course by then we would sleep in separate rooms, or else lay side by side in my big bed that I'd never rid myself of since Ed died, though I often thought of it, maybe holding hands, or he might touch my face with his fingertips, inquiringly, as it were. "I am well," I would whisper, and he would breathe gently in through his nose and turn on his side, away from me, companionably, as if we'd been married for many years and loved each other in a way the young know noth-ing about. Why do people not think that is a good way to be?

After the conversation with Alex's son ended, I said out loud, con-versationally, as if to alleviate the weight on my chest the news of Alex's death had brought, "There was a killing on my roof." I would have said "murder," but that is a word reserved for crows, (groups of ravens are an 'unkindness' – who makes this stuff up?) and any-way, it satisfied nothing and brought me no information. But still, the eye that refused to open into meaning for me, the ruffled wings, throat and tail, the glossy black body that, where it wasn't fat and full, was jagged and unkempt, all gave me the shivers, and I couldn't – I *could not* – believe that the encounter had been meaningless. But because the bird was so big and the incident so shocking, I felt it couldn't be an omen of merely the death of one old, ill person. I even wondered, in a more fanciful moment, if it could be signaling something as monstrous as an approaching terrorist attack on this oil-and-gas city. But I still couldn't shake off the amorphous tension, even dread, the raven incident had left me with.

Hadn't I loved the man? In those early months when he had come back from Toronto, hadn't I swooned for him like a sixteen-year-old girl? And years later when he got his diagnosis and left me to go back to where his children were so they could care for him, didn't I roll in my bed in an agony of longing for him? I blush to think of it. But still, the idea of an entire raven killing being required to bring me this news struck me as outlandish. After all, Alex had been gone from Calgary a couple of years; sometimes Parkinson's moves slowly and sometimes it doesn't, but I'm pretty sure that prophecy doesn't move backward. You'd always be right, but there would be no point in it.

Yesterday, my anthropologist son Herald, secondarily a compar-ative religionist, was in Calgary briefly in order to give a lecture at the university; this I found out only when he knocked unexpectedly at my door. His very arrival being something far out of the normal and causing me, at the same time, distress and something close to joy, I had to search about for something to say to him beyond the usual small talk. I asked him the meaning of the raven incident.

"Stop reading so much," he said. "You only upset yourself." He was wearing a queer electronic device hanging around his neck and when I asked him what it was for, he said, "I have developed an au-ditory disease and I am now nearly deaf and soon will be totally so."

To tell me such a thing without any warning at all! I don't imag-ine he could see any change in me at this news, but my heart skipped a beat or two (something it has begun to do now and then) and, for a minute, I had trouble getting my breath. He was once again my two-year-old boy I would do anything to protect. All I could think of, though I tried not to, was of the raven on my roof which had fixed me with that blank yet seeing eye.

Then Herald said, "I may as well tell you now, Mother, that I've been diagnosed with prostate cancer." I knew at once by the calm, even casual, way he told me that he was saying he had been given a death sentence, and I must say that I began to wonder why I was living so unpleasantly long, while he was dying at such an early age. Strangely, at this second piece of bad news, although I could hear the beat of my own heart in my ears, I seemed to have passed into another level of alertness and did not have to struggle for breath. Before I could respond, though, he changed the subject.

"You should know that I have a partner. His name is Tobias. He has been diagnosed with a rare, rapidly-moving, motor neuron disease, and has contacted one of those death groups. We talked about a suicide pact, but decided against it because I want to finish my book first, and he is already in crisis and must act as soon as possible. I'm not sure he will be there when I get back." How much he looked, at that moment, like his father, as Ed lay dying. I had to look away. "It's too bad," Herald went on, "because we had hoped to be there to nurse each other through to the end." A wave of pure pity swept through me, sorrow for my child – sorrow and pity I knew he would reject at once – he is my son, after all.

I said, "I will go back with you and nurse you."

He shook his head, no, firmly. "His demise is…was imminent. Mine is not."

Neither of us spoke about it again, but I could not, for the life of me, understand how we – mother and son – had come to this conversation. At the door, he leaned toward me to plant a dry kiss on one cheek. I clutched his arm, pulling him against me, but after a second, wrenching hard so that I lost my balance and almost fell, he wrested himself away from me.

After Herald's distressing visit, although harder for me than it used to be, I put on my coat, went outside, crossed the street to the park, and began to stroll the empty paths, empty because it was twilight on a frigid, late-fall day, and those who had something better to do – apparently nearly everybody – were off doing it. The park was hushed; I thought it an unnatural hush, but welcomed it for its near-magical beauty, as if the air itself had visible texture and the tiniest winking glitter throughout it, and because to be walking in beauty, like the poet said, was so precious and rare, even though I walked in only a small, city park, surrounded by multi-storey buildings, and a neglected park at that. And any of the personal beauty Byron was writing of had long ago departed from me.

I had entered into a denser part of the park, where the trees were bigger and older, and the fallen leaves coating the ground beneath them, once vibrant reds, oranges and gold, were dried and dusty, decaying at their edges and beginning to rot. Before too long, thoughts of Alex's death and Herald's approaching one began to leave me and my mind reached that space where there seem to be no thoughts at all. It was then that I saw a wolf squeezing its way out from a dark crevice in the base of a large deciduous tree at the edge of the path, and I thought, in quick fear, to stop walking, perhaps to turn back. But the wolf didn't even notice much less threaten me, and trotted off in the other direction, and thus my fear passed as quickly as it had come. The wolf paid no attention to me, it didn't appear dangerous; it seemed, if anything, to be companionable, more like a pet than a fearsome wild animal, as if, had it passed by you, you might safely reach out and stroke its thick fur. But later, when I was back home, its strange appearance in such an unheard-of way and in such a place where there are no wolves, made me pause, and consider carefully.

In the days when Herald was a young professor turning out papers and then books, he was careful to send me copies of his writings which, to his surprise, I always read, but he didn't know that I then went on to read more deeply in whatever area his most recent paper or book was about. Thus, I knew that wolves are, in Roman mythology, guardians, not proponents of evil as they are in most other mythologies, (although not in the Cree vision). In Norwegian myths, the monstrous wolf Fenris (or Fenrir) had to be chained in the bowels of the earth and when he breaks free, I have read – as apparently he is expected to one day do – he will devour the sun and cause the end of times.

Although the wolf I had just seen was of ordinary size and colour, as a prophetic animal he might indeed have been struggling his way up from the bowels of the earth, up through the roots of the tree and then emerging from a sort of slit in the trunk – not a cut, but a natural (or most unnatural) place that opened for him. I saw only darkness in the trunk and him twisting and pushing his way out. I knew even then that as an old woman my second sight was growing stronger: I was becoming better and better able to see the spirit world and I was indeed frightened, not by my ability, but by what I saw and all that I could no longer deny lay behind it.

In the weeks before the raven incident, the Americans, in a rage against 'the elites', (meaning anybody who knows anything – shades of the Red Guards!) elected a president whose ramblings, as well as being untruthful more often than not, frequently defied reason. I saw him as the purveyor of the original, many-formed mythological Lord of Chaos himself. Of course, I couldn't help but remember my dead husband Ed (who hated my saying things like "lord of chaos" as ridiculously excessive) in his later years, yelling at the television set, "Apocalypse Now!" (not that I think he had ever seen that film, and, as he didn't read, he certainly never read Conrad's *Heart of Darkness*). I suppose I told him about the connection and about the movie's version of Conrad's story. In any case, he certainly knew what it meant. I am in some ways glad that he died without ever seeing this president thing happening. It might have killed him.

But now, thinking yet again of the raven, for the first time in a concrete way, I faced directly the fact that Alex was the last of my lovers; he was my last lover in this life. I liked the sound of that; it gave his death dignity, I thought. I lived to testify that he was a good deal more than just another old geezer croaking his way into nothingness. I remembered again the nothingness in the bird's eye; that I stared at it as long as I dared and no spark of life came from it, although I knew it to be alive and capable of murderous aggression.

When I came back from my walk, I knew I was shielding myself from the meaning of what I had seen in the park, but I was tired out from the day and from Herald's visit, and was trying not to think about how I would probably never see him again, either. I fought with that knowledge, too: it weighed so very heavily on me, and my personal sorrows on the one hand, and the prophecies of the mythological world on the other, wrestled with each other, tormenting me.

I turned on the television news: War in Syria; terrorism in Turkey, Yemen, Iraq, Afghanistan, and spreading everywhere; an earthquake in Italy, or was it Chile or Peru? even one, startlingly, in Nunavut. Another mass shooting underway in the United States and one in France; cholera breaking out in Haiti and Bangladesh; wildfires consuming Israeli, Australian and Californian cities; the life-giving forests vanishing from South America and elsewhere; polar bears dying out in the north, icebergs melting, and the great birds everywhere being exterminated. But the wolf had seemed simple and harmless, absolutely unthreatening, and never even bothered to look at me.

Yet the legend of Fenrir says that because he looked normal and harmless, at first the gods allowed him to roam freely about the meadows. But legend said that this wolf was destined to kill the highest god Odin so they decided to bind him with chains and put him away in a safe place forever. Did they know that one day Fenrir would escape to swallow the sun? I thought then, only: *It has begun.*

PANSY

Inspired by Willa Cather's "Paul's Case", 1905

SINCE MY ACCIDENT LAST YEAR, I DON'T DRIVE ANYMORE. SO THE OTHER day, as I was trundling my ever-humiliating shopping cart home from the grocery store, as I waited for a green light, I found myself gazing idly down the traffic-clogged avenue all the way south to where it climbed a long hill, and at the peak abruptly disappeared from view. An intense longing pierced me, as if in my moment of unfocused reverie something I didn't know was in there had seized its chance to thrust its way into my solar plexus and on upward, fiercely, into my heart. The sensation, intense enough to be unendurable, weakened almost at once so that I could breathe, but in that brief time, the air had changed around me, and I could see the particles of light.

The signal changed to green then; I was able to collect myself enough to cross the street, grocery cart and all, and step up onto the sidewalk on the other side. But I had to go a few feet before the air smoothed itself out, and the din of modern city life returned to my hearing. How odd it was to me to identify this powerful but ill-defined hunger as homesickness, for in all my life I have never had a home. At least, not in the sense that other people do.

I suppose this was the real reason I decided to attend Gerry's funeral, not because I cared about Gerry, or for the sake of his wife Debbie, a girl with whom I'd once gone to school, or his kids whose names I don't even know. I never met one of them. By the time they married, I'd been gone from Auburn for years, having run away at sixteen, unable to wait another second for my real life to begin. At first I didn't keep in touch with anybody, but as the years passed, and maybe it was after my divorce from Aaron, I started sending the occasional Christmas card to my cousin, Roxanne, or a postcard to this or that school friend from wherever I happened to find myself. I'd begun to add a return address, just a postal box number in a nearby city, where I kept an apartment and eventually settled after my retirement. After that, people sometimes started to keep me up to date on what they were doing. That was how I knew, years ago, that Gerry had gotten re-married. But now I didn't even know what he had died of; an anonymous person had sent me the newspaper clipping about his death but it didn't say, and Roxanne claimed not to know. Probably the usual: cancer, heart failure, stroke, dementia. He was the most ordinary of men; I can't imagine him dying of some rare disease.

When I got out of my taxi at Roxanne's house, she was standing in her open doorway, leaning on a walker that held a small oxygen canister in its basket, the tubing running up her chest and clipping onto her nose. I hadn't seen her in at least twenty years, the last time when she was travelling and had dropped in to see me in Vancouver where I was then temporarily located, and I was shocked at the way she looked. It wasn't so much that she had put on weight as it was that she had lost any shape at all, as if her skin had stopped its job of restraining and shaping, so that she was more like an hourglass where gravity had pulled everything to the bottom. It looked like she had whole-body elephantiasis or, it occurred to me, was maybe wearing some heavy medical apparatus under her flowered muumuu. "Roxanne," I cried as I struggled up the wide front steps to the verandah and an arm that didn't appear to be attached to a person reached out from behind Roxie to hold the door open.

"Pansy!" Roxanne replied, her voice tremulous. When she hugged me, letting go of her walker for just one second, I could feel a minute but steady electrical tremor running through her arms and hands, as if her nerves had forgotten how to rest. But she smelled sweet, like a baby, and her smooth grey cap was neat and held back from her face with shiny pins, and I was relieved – to my own surprise – because I thought it meant she was getting good care, and having years ago done a doc on the mistreatment of elders, I am always sensitive to the possibility.

"This is Alice."

Alice, the rest of the body belonging to the arm, stepped out and, using her body to hold open the door, said, "Greetings, Mrs. Pomeroy! I hope your trip went well." She looked about sixty, and was dressed in gaudy runners, rumpled khaki pants and a green nurse's smock. She helped Roxanne back herself away from the door, and me to enter, taking my bag and saying, "I'll just run this up to your room while you get yourselves settled." This was easier said than done, at least for Roxanne, but never mind.

In that instant of greeting I had seen that Alice was old enough to remember me from my days as the host of a daytime television talk show, that she was just a bit intimidated to meet me. *The Pansy Pomeroy Show:* ten years it ran and the minute I got a wrinkle it was history. But that was quite a while ago now – my stardom and its accompanying power – so I'm frankly surprised when anybody remembers me, but this crisp little light still flicks on when they do, before it once again flickers out. Today my show would be called, maybe, just *Pansy Pomeroy*, or, *Pansy Pomeroy and Friends*, or *Pansy Pomeroy Talks!*

"Pardon?" We were seated across from each other, a polished coffee table between us, on matching pink sofas with leaf designs outlined in silver on them that looked brand new. I had to hope that Roxanne hadn't seen my smile.

"How was your trip?" she repeated in that same quivering voice.

"Ah! You know – crowded, ill-mannered people, smelly – oh, let's not be boring. How are you?" Her smile faded when I said this, and she looked down at her knees.

"As you see." Her tone was pleasant, as if we were discussing the weather. I had forgotten how annoying she always was in her goodie-two-shoes, Pollyanna-ish way. "I am dying, of course, Pansy." Oddly, she lifted her eyes from her knees to meet mine, and smiled at me as she spoke. "Let's not be cute."

"I was not being cute," I said, not meaning to sound injured. "I did not know. How is a person to know if she isn't told?" Roxanne was either suppressing a laugh, or a curse; I couldn't tell.

But, there it was again, the old back and forth; wanting to quarrel, trying not to, quarrelling anyway, two old broads with pills and their oxygen and their walkers – well, I was determined not to have a walker on this trip so I left it behind, and I am not on oxygen – and here we still are, sparring verbally. Now, there would have been a good name for my show: *Sparring with Pansy Pomeroy!* Oh, give it up. They are all stupid names for a non-existent television show.

"Well, I'm not," I said, meaning, not dying. Roxie opened her mouth but closed it again without speaking, pressing her lips together.

"I use a wheelchair when I go out, so I've hired a handicap van to take us to the funeral tomorrow," she said. It was my turn to purse my lips. "I'd appreciate it if you'd swallow your pride and ride with me."

"Of course, I will," I said. Some things can't be avoided; I've learned at least that over the years. When I divorced Aaron I had to face a lot of things, although I tried to get my lawyer to handle everything. *Pansy*, he said to me, *some things cannot be avoided.*

"How true that is," Roxanne said, laughing in a way that hovered between the wry and outright bitterness, and I realized I had said that bit about not being able to avoid some things aloud.

"I was thinking about Aaron," I said, aware how stiff I sounded. "Or rather, Charles."

"Charles?" She seemed puzzled.

"My second husband."

"Oh, come on, Pansy. I know he was your third."

I took a deep breath, not this again. "For god sake," I said. "We were married, what? Six, eight months?"

"I think it was more like two years."

"It was not."

After that we didn't say much for a bit; Roxanne fiddled with her oxygen tubing and I tried to think of something neutral to say. Then Alice brought in a tea tray complete with a plate of cookies and a glossy cake decorated with purple and yellow sugar pansies, at which I felt a twinge of something, or would have, but I was thinking of Charles, near the end when he was ill. Whenever we left the house he had to ride around in a wheelchair. Especially how he was in airports. The minute he hit the wheelchair and some attractive young woman paid to be charming would take charge of the apparatus with him in it, he would get the look on his face of a small child being taken care of by an attentive, loving mother – trusting, innocently smug, this captain of industry, this monster capable of such small, precise cruelty to his staff and his family –

PANSY

and seeing it, I would want to beat him on his overly-large head with my carry-on. Yet his kids, who were permanently in his thrall pretty much no matter what he did, kept on accepting his undeserved rage, his deliberately cruel sallies at them that he occasionally – if he was being nice – pretended was only wit.

I was his third and last wife; I got what was left after the children got their bequests, the goodies, you might say, and I have no guilt about it; I earned every penny. Both his ex-wives, women I didn't even know, tried to warn me not to marry him. I deliberately misunderstood them – thought they were merely jealous – but I should have listened. Whether I was willing to admit it or not, he was part of *the plan* that I'm beginning to see guided me from the day I realized that I was pretty enough and smart enough to make my way to the top. I hadn't reckoned on the necessity of luck. When I was young, I spat in the eye of luck.

"It's hard, isn't it," I said. Roxie looked up questioningly from the cake that she was cutting shakily with a china-handled, silver knife that must have been her mother's.

"Nothing special," I said. "Everything." She was carefully moving a slice to a tea plate. "No, that our mothers are dead." Now she was trying to lift the teapot to fill our cups, but she was taking so long that I realized that, full, it was too heavy for her. We didn't look at each other or speak as I poured and then sat back again.

"I think of mine every single day without fail," Roxanne said. "I cannot get her out of my head. It is the strangest thing, given that she has been dead for nearly forty years, and that I'm over eighty myself. I mean, do you think about Aunt Rebecca?" I was reluctant to give such a notion any credence, which Roxy must have known because she went on, "Of course, you didn't see her after you left home, did you?"

"I came to Auburn to see her when she was in the hospital," I said. "I was in the middle of a project. I had to get back right away. A lot of money and jobs were riding on that project." I sighed; it was sort of true. Roxie dropped her head as if it were too heavy to hold up. "I told her I'd come back in a few days, but when I finally managed to get things into shape so I could leave, she was gone. Stella and Bob were with her though." I added this last quickly. "They were always closer to her – you know that. And I came back for her funeral."

Now I was imagining getting up the church steps with the

wheelchair, but Roxy said, "I've arranged for one of the funeral di-
rector's staff to meet us at the lift so we don't have to worry about
the stairs."

"I can climb stairs perfectly well," I said.

"Honestly," she said, but that was all. A silence followed during
which I wanted to ask what had killed Gerry – if she knew – but I
was trying to think how to guide a conversation to where the answer would reveal itself without my having to ask, when out of the
blue, suddenly smiling at me, Roxy said, "I remember when you
wanted to be a ballet dancer."

She is the only one who knows that. When we were about
eight, other than her, only my mother knew of my foolish dream.
My mother, of course, was the first to label the notion foolish. It
was foolish because nobody, including me, had ever seen a ballet
dancer, never mind a ballet, and had no specific idea what a ballet
dancer actually did. It was then that her father and mine went into
a short-lived business together, our families were together a lot then,
and for that time, we became best friends. But then the business
went broke, there was some unpleasantness about it and we were
kept apart after that until my father died. So it was the pale tutu,
the taut, slender legs, the feet *en pointe* (although I would be an adult
before I knew that term) in the stiff satin slippers, the bare shoulders, and the glistening hair-covering which I would learn was called
by the unlovely name of *snood* that took my breath away.

I had seen the image of a dancer in a magazine of my mother's;
it was an advertisement probably selling face powder or something,
but all I saw was the grace of the pose, the long, slender fingers, the
meditative, almost sad expression on the face I would one day learn
to call "Botticelli." I wanted that. In an instant, after I'd recovered,
I knew that was what I wanted – whatever it was. But in my childhood, even if we had reached a city large enough for dance studios
and ballet teachers, I would have been too old. Modern dance, in
the world I had been born into, was mostly still laughed at. And
anyway, we were poor, a poor family, and how would lessons have
been paid for? Who would pay for the costumes?

Sitting across from my cousin Roxanne, once a pretty girl as I
too had once been, lithe and quick, slender as young trees, and now
lumpy, wrinkled, not so much overweight as misshapen, I saw that
I chased after that image all my life, wanting to live in the world it
represented where people did not have jobs or bosses, where boys

did not fumble and grope, and call you names if you asked for a little polish from them, where you did not spend your young womanhood washing dishes and diapering smelly babies. I wanted the lavish bouquet of roses the dancer would have in her dressing room and on the marble-topped table in her home, which would be all thick rugs, floating silk curtains, and soft light; I wanted the handsome men in tuxedos who surely wooed her; I wanted the theatre I had read about, the dazzling parties and balls, even the long cigarette holders, and false eyelashes and designer clothes. I did not want small, prairie villages with their uneducated louts (I more or less included my own family in this description), their wooden sidewalks, their dirt roads, their stupid kids who laughed if you said something smart in school they didn't understand. Sometimes your teachers didn't understand the things you said either, and gave you a puzzled smile and didn't say anything at all but moved on in a faintly confused way to the next child as if you hadn't spoken. I was nine years old when I saw the picture of the ballerina, and I wanted out: I wanted to be a ballet dancer; I wanted to be a famous actress or a famous author, and write books. I wanted above all to live in a sophisticated, glamorous world, and to be surrounded by nothing that was ugly, makeshift or second-hand or hand-me-down, but only the newest and the best. That I finally achieved this should have made me happy, and it did, sometimes. Mostly, I was grimly proud.

But if I had mentioned any of that then – no, if I said it today, the people I know would shrug their shoulders and say languidly, *who didn't*, and I imagine we'd laugh, if in a pained, inward way. When I was a child, an adolescent, a teenager, though, if I'd told people what I dreamt of they would have thought I was a crazy person, and they would mean the word 'crazy' literally. They wanted boyfriends and husbands, fellows with some land or good jobs in town, ones whose dads owned the drug store or the general store or the hardware store. They wanted a raft of babies – can you imagine? – they wanted nice little bungalows with front lawns and flower beds and a vegetable garden in the back. They wanted their parents' lives, only slightly nicer; they lacked any imagination at all. They did not want to be ballet dancers, or internationally known writers or painters, or even movie stars. They thought all that was silly – worse, they thought it was simply another universe from the one in which we lived, an uncrossable barrier existed between it and ours; to want it at all would be only to break your head and your heart; and it was all worthless stupidity, as any fool could see. I got away as fast as I could after my sixteenth birthday, I was out of there, I was history.

It occurred to me that I hadn't asked Roxanne a thing about her life.

"How do you pass your time?" I asked, trying to inject a little warmth into the question, as if I really cared what she did with her time.

"You mean, what do I do with myself, given the state of my debilitation?" Roxanne countered. I hesitated.

"The days are long," I said, then amended it to, "I find the days are long. How many books can a person read?"

"People drop in," she said. "I am getting my affairs in order. That keeps me busy for a couple of hours each day – putting loose snapshots into albums and labelling them, that sort of thing."

"For whom?" I asked.

"For Melinda," she said, and her voice was that of a little girl explaining to her mother why she'd cut a lock of her own hair, or painted on the mirror with her mother's lipstick.

"Of course," I said. "Dear Melinda. She was a sweet little girl." Not that I had a single memory of her as a child, but Roxy seemed, for once, not to have noted my untruth. What mother thinks her little girl isn't adorable? "It's a shame St. John's is so far away."

"Yes, a shame," Roxy whispered.

"In that regard, we have wound up in the same boat: no children to care for us in our old age. When everybody else was having babies I was making documentaries in countries we'd never even heard of when we were kids."

"And sending us postcards from them just to drive it home."

"Drive what home?"

"That you were living the good life, and we weren't."

The good life? Lying in sleeping bags on the floors of mud huts, beating off insects and snakes and all sorts of creepy-crawlies, spending weeks in places where we were surrounded by fly-ridden beggars, surly thieves, and would-be kidnappers, with machine-gun fire and bombs going off in the distance. Having to hire bodyguards. I still sometimes have nightmares about the things I saw in those years. But I had to spend some time on the dark side so I could build some credibility. I was pretty, but I wasn't *that* pretty – although I always pretended I was, and that mostly worked – and although I was smart, I was rarely quite as devious as I needed to be, until the later years that is. And wouldn't you know it, right about the time I was finally golden, age began to creep up on me; you can only fake youth for so long, you know, before people start to laugh at you.

"That was when I learned the final lesson."

"What?" Roxy asked. I had lost track of when I was musing and what I had actually said out loud, but I was aroused now, no longer quite in control.

"In the end you die, just like everybody else. You get old, and you die."

I realized now that Roxie's face had been in shadow ever since I had first seen her with her walker on the top step of the verandah of that rambling old house, doubtless slated to be torn down the minute she was gone and, built in its place, one of those stacked wood-and-glass boxes. I had not once seen her face clearly. Now, as she lifted her head at my remark and her eyes met mine, the light cleared it, I saw her face at last, and I saw how tired she was, tired of life, tired of being in pain, tired of being brave, tired of being a widow, tired of ungrateful children and dying siblings and dying friends, tired of being alone, tired of waiting for the end.

How clear her eyes were, so blue in that wrinkled, weary face; for a second, time unravelled, and I saw the girl in her again, her warmth and unfailing good nature, which I used to tease her about. She seemed to think being nice would spare her the misery from which we all suffer – as if life would not beat her even harder for it, beat some sense into her. I was so angry in those days.

Was she seeing me clearly too?

"Yes," I said, after a long time had passed. "You're right. Gerry Duncan and I were married for two full years before I left him. He trailed around behind me, him and his pathetic broken heart, for another year or so before he finally vanished. I went to Tokyo as a production assistant on my first documentary with that famous filmmaker whose name I can't even remember now. The company paid for my ticket, but it wouldn't pay for Gerry, and he couldn't afford to follow me. After that, he had gone somewhere when I got back to New York, and if I am to tell the truth", here I paused, laughing a little, "I never saw him again. And further, I did not miss him. I have not missed him once in fifty years. I have missed nobody; I have missed nothing."

Roxanne gazed steadily at me, the words she wouldn't say alive between us.

A roll of animal sound began low in my abdomen, in my womb: a ball of ripping claws tearing its way upward, the sound rising to a keening as it forced its way upward into my solar plexus, my chest, growing into a wail that rose and rose into a *howl* of the purest desolation. And I could not stop.

THE THINGS
THAT MATTERED

Inspired by Tim O'Brien's "The Things They Carried", 1990

FOR BREAKFAST, STILL PAYING HOMAGE MINDLESSLY TO A LIFETIME'S
habit of breakfast-eating, she ate bread spread with peanut butter.
Peanut butter was said to be nutritious and didn't require dishes or
turning on a stove. Studying the brown paste on the thin bread, she
knew that it was this or starvation, and the latter, she knew, would
come soon enough. Lately, food had become one of the things that
used to matter; the golden-skinned Christmas turkey, the cranberry
sauce, the mountain of whipped potatoes steaming in the bowl, yellow butter melting down its sides, or further back, the towering
wedding cake with its pink and white rosettes, the chocolate birthday cakes of her childhood, the roasts of beef and ham or red slabs
of salmon. Food only made her gut ache now; elaborate food bore
no more reality to her than a crumpled picture in a magazine did;
that she no longer felt hungry seemed to her inevitable and natural.
All her days now she sat in front of the television set, and wept.

At five p.m. she drank white wine, which did not stop the weeping, nor make it any worse. All evening as she sipped, she watched
the lanky women with the bony ribcages and too-prominent clavi-
cles, the awkwardly-long legs, like no people she could recall ever
having seen anywhere, who were, nearly all of them, blond, and

whose faces became increasingly indistinguishable from the one another. Understanding about Botox, facial surgery, electrolysis, breast enhancement, daily body-shaping workouts in gyms, bulimia, and anorexia, she wept. She remembered Chinese foot-binding, Japanese comfort women, female genital mutilation. Even while the women laughed their bright laughs and tossed their golden tresses, she wept for them, she wept for the women. She didn't let her thinking go any further because, although she wept all day each day, she did not want to sit and think of the vast and ancient cruelties of the world. She wept instead at what she saw.

And yet, the night that she heard, at three or four a.m., on her bedside radio, that an old woman's body had been found in her house in Rotterdam and that it had been there for ten years without anyone noticing the woman's absence, she had not wept. She felt wonder that the world could still surprise her, but then she filed that observation away along with thousands of others she had accumulated over the years. What a backlog, when you thought of it: a century of perceptions, insights, enlightening (although miniscule) glimpses of the fabric of the universe.

And in the world itself, insights available to all going as far back as Gilgamesh. Now don't get clever, some distant part of herself reminded her. *It availeth naught.* She even wondered about that. How did she know if it did or didn't *availeth*?

Hadn't she seen enough of the brilliant ones whose faces repeated themselves day after day on the television set while she sat before them watching, listening intently, tears leaking steadily from her eyes, dampening her cheeks, their words constructed into sentences so cleverly that they made her weep, and still nothing of the world changed? While she suspected them of loving the words' sounds and their facility with them most of all? Not that it mattered anymore.

In any case, she had her standards. Having discovered, or so she thought, the shocking unreality of reality television, she didn't watch reality shows at all, nor the more vulgar of the half-hour sitcoms that actually, she discovered, lasted at the most only around twenty minutes, this seeming to her another in an endless line of hypocrisies big or small which made up the knitted threads of the world. She always muted the commercial messages, although she watched the screen with interest thinking how ingenious the scriptwriters were, even those who wrote the most loutish of the sitcoms, in being able to tell a story visually in so short a time, while their real purpose was only to sell the products in the advertisements. She was saddened at her lack of originality on this issue, and wished that she had been gifted with a bigger brain or one capable of more complex thought. She wondered if maybe they were the same thing but decided probably not. It was the sort of thing she could never talk to Mervin about.

Sex scenes annoyed her, though, to the extent she could still be annoyed about anything. They annoyed a part of her that had once mattered – that was it – but that nowadays was more a hazy recollection of annoyance than the real thing. Her once-normal sex life had ended with Mervin's death, whenever that was, and while for a number of years, as far as she could remember, this lack had been the source of the worst pain (again, she was not sure what that pain had felt like), it had been one of the first of the things that *had mattered* to simply melt away. At first this failure of its mattering had worried her a great deal, that she was abnormal both to want and not want its return, until its *not mattering* overcame the mattering and seemed both touching in some sweet way (or what she would once have called sweet) and inevitable and right, as breathing remained inevitable and right.

Her name was Velma York and she no longer knew for sure where her children were, although her eldest son had graduated from Harvard. When she had last seen her youngest son, he had just finished his training at a technical school, and was a plumber in this same city where she sat all day in front of the television set and wept – the children dug out of rubble from bombings, their tiny bodies as flexible as rubber, caked in a choking, grey clay, silent and merely acquiescent in their rescue. Or the African women refugees forced by human traffickers to work as prostitutes for as long as their bodies lasted; the African Americans who wept over their once-vigorous, laughing sons shot dead in the street; the Vancouver drug addicts responding to their questioners with a jaunty discomfort designed to hide their despair and shame. Or even the desiccated hides of elephants killed only to satisfy the ivory trade, their bodies rotted away, their outlines, like archeological discoveries of the foundations of once great palaces, all that was left. Her eyes were like wounds, seeping tears instead of blood; she barely needed a tissue, she didn't even sniffle. Hadn't someone once said that the wound is the eye or the eye is the wound? Or that the wound and the eye are one? Who was that? Jung? No, Hillman. But she wondered about wisdom: did tiny, penetrating insights advance the human species incrementally, since almost no one listened to them. Or, if they did listen, did humans understand them? Was her soundless weeping a response to that void?

Her child-rearing days had been so long ago though, that she felt nothing when she thought of her boys, having expended all her fruitless longings for them and then her grandchildren – surely now parents themselves. She remembered them more as dreams of her own or as happenings from another, different, world, fading closer to nothingness with each passing year. She had even stopped wondering why her boys had slowly abandoned her. As far as she could remember, she had been a reasonable and loving parent, as had Mervin been. But, it seemed, having all the time in the world in which to consider, that children all grew away from their parents and, given the right conditions, such a thing could happen as had happened to her boys with regard to her. They had simply not tried to arrest what was a natural inclination. She said out loud, testing this idea, "It was ever thus." She saw how true it was, but also how it wasn't always true. She thought this thought was something sensible over which she might weep, but she did not, not as she once had wept. She could think how ungrateful children were, as she supposed she had been with her own parents. But that memory went too far back, and her recollections of her own childhood were, nowadays, mostly pale and uncertain, bereft of all emotion, no longer mattering.

She recalled that for a few years, long ago, she had consoled herself with the notion that one day her grandchildren would look for her, until it occurred to her that they probably thought she had been a monster to her children, and then some time after that, she realized that they had probably been told she was dead. *What brave new world is this?* she had asked herself that day, meaning, a world in which the families of her youth had been curtailed and the world thus transformed to one she could not grasp. She discovered that her own childhood and her children now belonged to the expanse of floating shades of things that once had mattered, but no longer did.

Even, she thought, her weeping was suspect, so she examined it as well as she could. As far as she could tell it was spontaneous and not connected to a belief system about how the world was. She had never wept before in so general a way, not even when she had gone through a time when she had been somewhat less than 'deeply' religious: sort of mediocrely religious, a tentative believer waiting for the miracle that would sweep her into a life of self-abnegation and prayer; the vast, silent wind that touched only her as she knelt at the altar, the electric warmth shooting down her arm as she held her rosary, the ray of brilliant light from deep in the universe striking her and her alone, knocking her prostrate. After a while, when nothing of the kind happened, she had stopped with the religious stuff. She thought, *when you are religious, all you think about is yourself.* That was, as far as she could remember, when the weeping had begun.

Oh, probably not. It could have begun long before she had even noticed it herself.

And still, she thought, I do not close my eyes, I do not look away, and wondered why she hadn't the slightest urge to do either of these things no matter what she saw on the television set: a man being burned alive, a beheading, body parts from bombings spread across a café or a nightclub. It was perhaps that...she had to think. Could it be that such things didn't matter when you thought about the long sweep of human history? But she had always hated to think of the long sweep of human history; in her own life – that was all she cared to think about – in her own life all the killing had never stopped. How could it matter?

When Mervin died, although she had had her doubts about him, and also about their *very long* marriage, she had wept copiously. But, she thought, it was a different kind of weeping than that which she suffered now as she sat and watched the television set. That kind had involved her gut and her muscles; it had made her nose run until so much effluent collected in the back of it that it dribbled down her trachea so that she couldn't get breath past it and she choked and coughed. It was, she could recall, a horrible kind of weeping, although surprisingly satisfying at the time. As if the gallons of tears were reaching into every single cell in her body in order to wrestle out the poison of being alive; the stone that boy had thrown in second grade that had cut her forehead and made blood flow widely down her face so that everyone thought she must be dying and she couldn't stop screaming until her mother slapped her; the day she realized that Mervin had had a silly affair right under her nose and, even though he had stopped by the time she found out, she had struck him hard in the centre of his chest with her closed fist and he had walked away, and they never spoke of it again. Those memories were being washed out of her cells, too. And more, a thousand, thousand more things about their marriage and before that, her childhood and her young womanhood, her middle age, her early old age, were being washed out by that violent crying, leaving her, as far as she could recall, feeling weak and warmish, as if she had a mild fever, and her muscles like fish flopping uselessly in too-shallow water.

The morning she had heard on the radio that not far from where she lived, an eighty-five-year-old husband had murdered his eighty-three-year-old wife, she was surprised enough that for a second the weeping stopped. What was that saying about all passion spent? Milton, was it? Must have been, everything that wasn't Shakespeare was Milton. Was the weeping because all her passion was spent? Again she laughed inside: as if living, breathing humans could finally expend their way out of all passion. Not even Buddhist monks, she told herself, then wondered if that was true. Although there could be no doubt, at least in her experience, that passion too, faded year by year until there was only this weeping left. Maybe the old man had a brain tumour. Maybe he had dementia, and thought his wife was an intruder, like that too-handsome footless athlete in South Africa, or someone evil coming to kill him. Maybe he was evil. At this thought, she became aware again of the water leaking from her eyes. Not individual tears, but a gentle bath of warm water so near the same temperature as her skin and flesh that she could barely distinguish it from herself.

She wondered what possible use her weeping could be. Then she wondered if her weeping was real; then she wondered what real was. She knew if she ever told anyone, not that there was anyone to tell, they would think her an idiot and probably also a liar, or one so *self-involved* she couldn't tell real from not real. Real: no intermediary between what she saw and what happened in her eyes. But what were her eyes connected to? Nerves. Muscles. What Schopenhauer – wasn't it Schopenhauer? – called intellect, meaning the physical body, and said that women were only capable of sensation. She gave up on that line of thought as it told her nothing, and was probably nonsensical besides, although she did like her own idea: the lack of intermediary between herself and what she saw on the television set. No perfectly coiffed hair and made-up face with the constantly moving mouth, no husband's opinion, no sons' opinions, no friends' opinions. No opinions of her own either, after so many years of working to have opinions – another of the things that *used to matter* – no thoughts about what she saw. Sometimes pictures came floating up of the years when she and her women friends, otherwise left alone in the world, had played at being bold and cheerful, travelling everywhere together, serving each other gourmet dinners, shopping, and going to movies, plays, and concerts together. Where had that all gone? Faded away with Parkinson's diagnoses, Alzheimer's, dropsies of various kinds, not to mention arthritis, heart problems, and brain aneurysms. Could it be that now, even her once-profound need for companionship had stopped mattering?

Since Alma had gone into hospital and not come out, Alma being the last of those people she had known for more than fifty years, no one dropped in for coffee now and then. Thus, even the morning after she had wakened in the middle of the night with a mild heart attack there had been no one to tell. It had become too difficult to get to a doctor, and anyway, no doctor would take that short-lived, moving pain from chest to arm to shoulder and then back to the centre of the chest with any degree of seriousness; she would only be shamed as a foolish old woman looking for attention. At the time, though, her heart attack hadn't been what she had been led to believe it would be like: agony combined with terror, that sort of thing. It had been interesting, especially the part near the end where she began to feel the heavy pressure on her chest and had realized that if you examined that sensation carefully, you would see that it wasn't really a heavy weight *on* her chest but something going on *in* her chest. This ability to locate and identify her bodily sensations, she recalled vaguely, must have come from the years she had done yoga and meditated. When was that? She couldn't recall, or couldn't be bothered to recall. Unfortunately, the sensation of weight hadn't lasted long enough for her to get to the bottom of it, which had disappointed her. This thought made her laugh, not on the outside so anyone would notice, but inside, she was laughing. And still the water passed softly from her eyes down her cheeks.

Once she had been on the phone with an old friend of Mervin's whom she had always liked, when a heart attack had struck him. She heard him fall, heard the phone hit the hardwood floor, heard his groans and gasps, and the footsteps of his daughter as she came running to him, and her cries of alarm before the phone went dead. Velma was left with the indelible memory of what such a death sounded like. Yet she could not feel fear for herself; it seemed she had passed beyond fear too, although water leaked steadily from her eyes.

Maybe she wept from loneliness. But she did not long anymore for anything; she no longer thought (and hadn't for a long time) that she would die of grief, or of loneliness, or of longing. Something would kill her; she had only to wait to find out what it would be. Perhaps it would be the weeping itself. The old kind of weeping made her clearer about whatever it was she was weeping over; it dissolved the poisonous residue left in all her cells by her human re-lations, but *this* weeping – no, there could be no doubt about it – was making her smaller and smaller, as if things, the world, were simpler than she had ever thought they could be. Not clearer, but slowly fading together, the edges of each once separate thing blur-ring and smudging. Weeping here in front of the television set, day by day, she began to understand that she too melted a little; each day a little more of her dissolved.

At night, as she lay there in bed, the darkness relieved only by the glow of the radio's dial, she began to wonder who had been paying the taxes on the house of that woman whose body had been found in Rotterdam; who had been paying the heat and light and water bills. Or, when the old woman had died, had her taxable-cit-izen self also died, been wiped from the city's tax rolls by the invis-ible hand of that economist of ages past? It did not seem possible, because after all, Velma had seen how, as a social being – that is, as a part of her society – one could die utterly as she seemed herself to have done, and no one would notice, but she had never thought it possible that her legal self would not live on, even ten years after her physical death.

Was it even in Rotterdam that it had happened? Maybe it was Raleigh or Richmond or – she found she couldn't think of any other cities beginning with 'R.' Reykjavik, Ravenna. They all melted to-gether into one city full of old women, grieving yet patient, weeping in front of television sets. Reims, Rouen. All those cities in Asia, Africa, and the Middle East with names she couldn't pronounce or spell and had never seen. Riyadh. Regina. Rivière-du-Loup. What would it matter, she began to wonder, if one died and one's body was not found for ten years?

Her chest had begun to ache gently, and the water seeping from her eyes had grown even warmer so she could feel it now heating her face as it flowed bountifully down, sluicing gently off her cheeks and chin, flooding onto her chest where it was soaking her garments, its tide warming even her arms and hands and knees, legs and feet. It was dissolving her as always, but now, instead of finding herself growing smaller and smaller, she felt some fragile, surprising change swimming through her cells; she felt herself beginning to expand, filling the room, the house, spilling through the empty city streets, spreading onward out into the countryside, her now liquid self blending with rivers as she crossed them, sliding silently through the limbs and trunks of spruce and pine forests, on and on over the jagged blue mountaintops, the ice-filled crevasses, the shining glaciers until finally, the burden that was herself, the burden of being alive, now liquefied, melded peacefully into the sea.

GUILT: A DISCUSSION

Inspired by Shirley Jackson's "The Lottery", 1948 and
Flannery O'Connor's "A Good Man is Hard to Find", 1953

BARBARA'S SON ALAN HAD PLACED HER HERE A FEW YEARS AGO WHEN IT
was agreed, even by her, that she could no longer handle the house
she had been living in for the last twenty or so years. He had been
tentative and presented his case carefully, pointing out that his sister
Alana, who lived in Florida with her third husband (Meredith, his
second sister was dead, and his half-sister Jessica was never mentioned), and Barbara's younger brother George, who lived with his
wife of more than fifty years in Vancouver, had come to this consen-
sus as well. She had seen it coming though, maybe even five years
earlier, but, recognizing the inevitable, was not of a mind to put up
a fight even though she deeply dreaded such a move – who wouldn't,
it being the end of all autonomy, ninety-nine per cent of one's dignity, and one hundred percent of anyone else's respect for you?

"You're so resilient, Mom," Alan said, seeming genuinely ad-
miring. How she loved that boy, if nowadays through a thin scrim
consisting of what she couldn't say: the distancing she knew she
needed to survive his foreseeable (maybe even Nature or God-de-
signed) indifference. Putting the useless and energy-consuming old
out on the ice floe and all that. Reasonable, probably deserved.

"Four walls and a roof," she told him, flipping one hand dismis-
sively. "Why do people get so worked up about moving?" She knew

perfectly well, if he didn't: downsizing was saying the final good-bye to a full and rich life; it meant setting one foot out, tentatively, in profound grief, into one's very grave. But no use saying that. Grimly, when he had gone, she muttered to herself, *I deserve no better*. The arrangements, she was certain, had already been made before he came to ask her about the move.

"I often think," Sherry was saying now, as the four of them – Barbara, Sherry, Jessie-Marie and Sonya – sat around the table in the common room sipping tea and playing a desultory game of hearts, "that I must have been just about the worst mother you could possibly be."

"Oh, no," Jessie-Marie said, raising her index finger and her eyebrows, without lifting her eyes from her cards, "I reserve that title for myself. The things I did; the things I missed; the crazy ideas I had."

"Ough!" Sonya declared. "We all had and thought and did; that's how we were raised. At least we were better than our own crazy parents."

"And yet," Barbara said, "here we all are." Snorts of laughter or disgust or maybe even despair went round the table. Sherry extracted a tissue from her sleeve and dabbed it briskly, once, against each eye. Sometimes they spoke of the pleasure they found in being together, but mostly they communicated this through meaningful glances and the occasional touching of hands.

"I offer as a prime example, my name," she said. "I mean, I ask you: I'm ninety years old and answer to the child-name Sherry."

"You could change your name," Barbara suggested. The table fell silent; cards were set down, the women looking around at each other.

"What an extraordinary idea," Jessie-Marie said. "I've changed my hair colour I don't know how many times over the years. I've had everything – black as Paulette Goddard's, blond as Marilyn Monroe's, red as Rita Hayworth's in *Gilda*. Why not your name?"

"*Gilda* was in black and white," Sonya said. Before anybody could speak, she added, "I know, I know. Everybody knows – she was *famous* for her fabulous mane of dark-red hair. God she was beautiful."

"I changed my last name three times," Jessie-Marie said. "We all changed our last names at least once. Except for you, Sherry. Was it four times for you?"

"No bitchiness," Barbara said.

"Why not?" Sonya asked.

"Don't you want to go to your grave with as few blots on your record as possible? I mean, isn't it time to try to be good?" Barbara didn't mean this, but thought she would try it out on this recalcitrant and godless bunch of old babes, who were her only friends. Babes!

"Like we have a choice," said Sonya, and it made them all laugh, the card game nobody had wanted to play in the first place, although they did so every late afternoon, forgotten.

"I would change it to...hmmm...maybe...Arabella? Jacinthe? Jasmine? No, maybe Rosalyn. I like that. Rosalyn." Heads nodded around the table, along with murmurs of agreement. "It has some dignity," Sherry-Rosalyn went on, "without being too complicated or unusual."

"God forbid an old lady should be unusual." Barbara again. "I am so effing bored," she said, pushing away her cards, smacking her palm against the table-top. "I am so effing bored I could kill myself."

"What happened to your famous resignation," Jessie-Marie muttered, but loudly enough to be heard by all. "The one you are always counselling us."

"I've tried it all," Barbara said, restraining herself with red-faced effort from shouting. "All the philosophers, several of the religions, the occasional self-help guru. And I am still bored."

She stated the latter so menacingly, through gritted teeth, that, Barbara noticed, the others seemed relieved when the attendant appeared at Sherry-Rosalyn's elbow, and began to pull her wheelchair back from the table. Funny how at a certain point an attendant always showed up. *When my face turns red*, Barbara acknowledged. Just as well. She did not like the enforced seclusion, which only made her angrier, or the tranquillizers which upset her bowels. *I have the right to be angry if I want to be.* Lord knew there was no point in knowing that; she had acquiesced to having-no-right when she had agreed to Alan's proposal of a move. *Proposal, my foot* – his thinly-disguised ultimatum.

The women took the attendant's arrival as a sign that it was time for all of them to disperse.

"Don't forget," Sherry-Rosalyn called, "my room, eight tonight." They sat at different tables at dinner, never knowing where the staff might put them, the idea being, evidently, that a change was as good as – what? Surely not a rest. A change might liven up their lives? Keep them alert? In Barbara's opinion, what it led to was a desperate, often angry, silence. In fact, she had noticed that some were never moved as they seemed to get too upset, not angry, but frightened when they had to sit in a different chair – but the chairs were identical! – with strange faces around them. But, having thought of this so many times, her mind moving in grooves, which she tried with every single ounce of her being to grind herself out of, nonetheless, she found herself brought to it again, and she gave in and thought once more how it seemed that spending more money on a more expensive facility got you nowhere, just to fancier surroundings, everything else being the same.

Tonight it was Sherry-Rosalyn's turn to choose the question. She lay stretched out on her neatly-made-up bed with the flowered quilt, her shoes off and her banged-up lumpy feet revealed in all their aged splendor, her back supported by several pillows. The rings on her gnarled fingers shot rainbows when she moved her hands. Jessie-Marie had seated herself carefully in Rosalyn's wheelchair, checking first to make sure the brakes were on. Too often somebody forgot to put the brakes on the wheelchairs and the 'guests,' trying to get into them by themselves, fell and broke legs or hips. At their ages, broken hips were curtains, and everybody knew it. Barbara, observing Jessie-Marie, could feel herself getting angry again. She had begun to believe that certain staff members did it on purpose. For all she knew, maybe it was a company policy: when a resident got too old, or too difficult – she had better watch out – or too senile and didn't want to move or the family didn't want to move the resident, the staff just quietly figured out a way to get rid of them. Or was she merely paranoid, another characteristic of too many of the aged, as Alan had told her when she raised the possibility of a murderous conspiracy. Jessie-Marie had applied a touch of lipstick, a hint of blush, and wore her dangly gold earrings, which gleamed when she turned her head.

Barbara was stretched out comfortably in Rosalyn's only arm-chair, the foot-rest out, her feet still encased in her shiny white slippers, relics from God knew where – those years in Florida, no doubt, which for reasons even she couldn't name, she rather treasured – and Sonya sat on the straight-backed parlour chair. Her back was bad, she needed the support, but her position in her stiff white cotton blouse gave her a prim, private-schoolgirl look. Barbara noticed that Sonya had put on her good necklace, the garnet one that her first husband had bought her forty years ago on a holiday in Cancun, just before he left with the floozy, the bimbo – but they had agreed not to use such words – the younger woman. In this light the necklace looked opulent although truly, it was only a trinket.

"Question. Question. Question." The word went round the room.

Rosalyn gazed at the ceiling, waiting for that hush that fell when all had readied themselves at last. They sat motionless, all involuntary tics and habitual shrugs and nods stilled, all breathing as gently as possible, all focusing on the room's possibilities: the room itself, or the air in the room, the very particles that made up the air. The pure spirit present in the room – always present, but rarely if ever felt, and never acknowledged – had begun to come through and past the wounds in the air – the pain, the anguish, the grief, even the rage – the very particles of hush crowding them all right out the door. Barbara could feel the heat rising in her pale cheeks, and see the cheeks of the others taking on a glow beginning to touch like tiny star-pins their faded, thin hair, and the darkness – oh, such welcome darkness – coming into their dulled eyes.

When all of them could feel that they had reached the required state – they could feel it but they could also hear it, or perhaps it was the absence of all other sounds that they heard now – Rosalyn cleared her throat, softly, and spoke.

"What was your greatest transgression?"

Was it Barbara's imagination, or were some other unseen presences with soundless *swishes* ranging themselves around the sides of the room, hidden in the shadows? Or were these new presences themselves the very shadows? Did the others hear or feel it? She couldn't tell.

Sonya gave a snort. Apparently it was her turn to start.

"When I was into my last week in my own house, I was deliberately profligate with the earth's resources." She emphasized "deliberately" and especially "profligate." "I had a hot bath every single morning. I filled the tub. I used a whole bottle of bath soap that week. It was…"

"You savoured it," Jessie-Marie whispered, and the shadows – were they giggling?

"Every second. I knew once I came here baths would be rare, not private, not pleasurable ever again. Just – necessary. Just – allowed."

"Such a terrible crime," Barbara said, smiling at her friend.

"But truly," Jessie-Marie pointed out, "none of us are climate-change deniers. We know that even though individuals don't have the power to make laws, in the end what will work will be when each of us takes responsibility for our actions." She hesitated. She had once been a lawyer, many, many years ago. "Vis-à-vis our destruction of the planet."

"And after all," Sherry-Rosalyn pointed out, "what sensual pleasures are there left to old women? Of the raft of them there once were: holding a baby, smelling its sweet baby-smell, feeling its warmth and heft against your chest and neck; eating all sorts of delectable things like Christmas cake and lobster and crème caramel that would kill us now...."

"Making love," Barbara said.

"Feeling the beauty of a male chest...."

"His back, his shoulders..."

"The orgasm itself," Barbara said, knowing perfectly well that as usual she had gone too far.

"I think," Sherry-Rosalyn said, "that it would be wise to stop this right now. All true..." she held up a hand to stay their objections, "but you know we have agreed that the purpose of these meetings isn't to wallow in what we have lost." Murmurs of agreement whispered around the shadowed room and the unseen presences rustled and murmured with them. Were they maybe only the dead of the nursing home? No, had to be more than that, Barbara insisted to herself.

"We had our time," Sonya said. "We had it and it was...beyond precious...beyond beautiful. But...it...is...over."

"Agreed." They spoke as one voice.

"Your turn, Jessie-Marie."

Jessie-Marie didn't hesitate a second; this wrongdoing, whatever it would turn out to be, had to have been on her mind for a long time. "When my son Anders got his girlfriend Jane pregnant and they were so young, both only eighteen, I think it was, and her mother and father were pressuring Anders to marry Jane at once..." She paused to swallow and catch her breath. "And his dad, Gerald was dead set against them getting married and threatened to punch out Janie's father if he didn't shut up..." she paused again, "I did nothing. They came to me, alone, because I wasn't offering advice or screaming at them, or demanding they do what I said. They came to me. 'Mother,' Anders said. 'Jane and I don't know what to do. What should we do? Should we get married? Should Jane have the baby and we not get married? Should we give the baby away? Should Jane have an abortion?' We were Catholics, you know. And getting an abortion was very, very hard to do in those days. It would have to be illegal and it would cost. Or else we would have to send them to another province where things weren't quite so backward. And that would be iffy."

"Why didn't they just get married?" Sherry-Rosalyn asked.

"At eighteen? They wanted college, they wanted adventure – oh, you don't need me explaining it."

"So what was your transgression in this?" Barbara asked briskly. They could all hear the lump that was the prelude to sobbing, which had risen into Jessie-Marie's throat.

"I...said...nothing. I had nothing to say. I was...paralyzed. Everything I thought of seemed wrong; I had no idea how to help them. I just sat and stared at them. I could feel my face getting hot, there was buzzing in my ears, my heart was thumping away in my chest and I felt...I couldn't breathe; I was afraid I was going to faint. Anders took my hand but I pulled it away from him." She made a gesture with one hand, pulling it back as if it had touched something sharp or too hot. "We sat there, the three of us, staring at each other. Jane began to cry. Tears ran down her face, but she didn't make a sound. Anders waited, but then, finally, he gave me such a look." Jessie-Marie had dropped her head, her shoulders narrowed and her torso had slouched; she was diminished, smaller, so tiny. So old. "They got up and went out of the room. They hardly made a sound leaving. And neither of them looked back, once, at me." For a moment, no one spoke, trying to absorb this.

"Don't you get it?" Jessie-Marie said, looking around at each of them. "I took no responsibility. I refused to help them. I didn't even talk with them about it. And Anders never came close to me again. That was my punishment. I have been punished for my cowardice, my selfishness, for as good as saying that it wasn't my problem, for all these many years."

"It sounds to me," Sherry-Rosalyn offered, "that you were very angry with them for being so utterly stupid as to get pregnant and ruin their own chances. You didn't feel that you should be cleaning up their mess."

"What were you?" Barbara asked. "Maybe forty at the time? What the hell did you know?"

"Which is what?" Jessie-Marie asked, angry now.

"About life," Sonya said, her voice gentle. "How could you know then that any one of the options would have been okay – unless you objected to abortion itself. We didn't know then that women have such trouble...."

"Some women," Barbara interjected, seeing where the conversation was going.

"...have trouble getting over abortions and even sometimes regret them terribly. You know, Jessie-Marie, as well as I do, that –"

"Things have a way of working themselves out?" Sherry-Rosalyn interrupted angrily. "As if they would have listened to that. Anyway, haven't we agreed already more than once about that as a stupid platitude?"

"But things do," Sonya pleaded. "They do."

Barbara felt she could hear whispered assent coming from the shadowed corners. "They certainly do something," she said. "So what happened that you are still troubled by this now?"

"What happened isn't the point. Isn't that another thing we've agreed on? That we would stick to the issue, not mix it up with other issues?"

"Do you feel any better for having told us this mistake?" Sherry-Rosalyn asked. She seemed genuinely curious.

"I'm not sure," Jessie-Marie admitted. "I lost my youngest son over it, so I can't just forgive myself as if it were nothing."

"Look. Here's the thing," Barbara said, exasperated. "You can't change it. You've suffered for fifty years over it. What do you think the gods require of us? We're only human beings!"

"Take it easy, Barb," Sherry-Rosalyn said. Once again the women fell into a listening silence, except for Barbara. "I guess it's my turn now."

"How did it get to be your turn?" Barbara inquired. She didn't like it when people tried to be leaders, whether they were good at it or not. That wasn't the point.

"Pay some bloody attention, Barbara," Sonya said. "You're always getting side-swiped by your own rage – or whatever it is – and thus, you are forever getting lost. It's Sherry-Rosalyn's turn because last time she was second and we work down the list. Next time she'll be fourth."

This explanation made little sense to Barbara (though she had to admit that Sonya was probably right; it was just that she never could be bothered with lists, and orderly arrangements, all that simply enraged her) and so she didn't argue. But the rage she was feeling, it struck her, explained why she had once been such a hard drinker. *Admit it, an alcoholic.* It explained too, why her first husband (she always referred to him as What's-His-Name) had left her and taken their little girl with him. She had been angry *before* he took their baby. And didn't she turn out all right? Jessica, Jessica, Jessica. *But I had other children after: Alana, Meredith, and last and best, Alan.* The truth was, she couldn't recall where Jessica lived now, although she had some vague memory of being told she was married and had children and lived in – was it Halifax?

"Okay," Rosalyn said, a little too comfortably for Barbara's taste. She couldn't get a read on the unseen presences gathered around the walls and in the corners. "I'm ready."

"Go," Jessie-Marie said. They took a second to settle themselves again. Barbara had to admit, yet another thing she had to admit, that she tended to be a disquieting presence. Her own mother had always been accusing her of some such a thing: *a bloody little demon. My demon daughter.*

"Yes, I am the one who changed my last name a total of four times: I was born Bradstreet and had three husbands, whose surnames were: Bodley, Newhouse, and Knight." She paused, smug as hell.

"We don't need to know their names," Sonya pointed out. Rosalyn, lost in her story, ignored her.

"I cheated on all of them." There was a startled silence. "I was a serial philanderer."

"But you had – how many children?" Jessie-Marie's voice was thin and high.

"Yeah, well," Rosalyn responded. She didn't look a bit as if she felt guilty.

"That is quite a transgression," Barbara said. "I mean, once, but –"

"Oh, I lost count," Rosalyn said. "I was a pretty woman, as you know. In my youth people even said I was a beauty. Not that that had anything to do with it. I just liked men."

"So why present this as a transgression then?"

"Wasn't it?" The answer being obvious, nobody replied.

"But you're not sorry," from Sonya. She turned to the others. "Do we have to be sorry? We do, don't we?"

Rosalyn said, "Nobody said anything about being sorry."

"Are you sorry? Even a bit?" Barbara asked.

"I liked the excitement, the plan-making, the huge risk. I liked that. Getting into bed with a new man – oh, wow, what a thrill that was. I never got over it. Until I got so old no man would look at me."

"So that's what you're sorry about?"

Rosalyn sighed heavily, turning her head away from them to gaze into the far corner of the room where the shadows were deepest. Suddenly Barbara understood that Rosalyn knew, just as she did, that the spirit-souls were there.

"You know I could say plenty of wise things to you: How I shattered any possibility of deeper relationships in my marriage; how I was distracted from my husbands, and also, I have to admit it, from my children. How I neglected things – the laundry, milk for the breakfast cereal, always being late for school pick-ups. All that... quotidian stuff."

"Hah!" Barbara said in surprise. "You were searching for, I don't know, immortality? "No, escape from our puny stupid suburban civilization."

"I just liked new sex," Rosalyn said, and everybody groaned at her, disgusted. "Oh, all right. What I feel isn't so much guilt, as...puzzlement. I mean, where did I get such an idea in the first place? Why did I get addicted to it? What the hell is the matter with me that I still can't honestly feel guilty? That's the question." She pointed a quivering forefinger at them as if they were the guilty ones.

"You felt superior to everybody else in your circle. It made you feel superior to everybody else caught in the daily meat-grinder of middle-class life." Jessie-Marie sounded a little too certain.

"Was that my sin?" Rosalyn asked in wonderment. "Maybe it was." She had begun to tremble, her grotesque little feet bounced gently on the flowered quilt.

"Is she having a stroke?" Barbara asked, and tried to get out of the big chair in which she had relaxed too deeply.

"I'm all right," Rosalyn said. "I was just...some things came back to me. I...we'll have to address this again another time when we need a new question." Nobody argued.

Barbara was beginning to wonder if this attempting to come to terms with their biggest sins was such a good idea, remembering the time the question had been about their greatest sorrow, and dead babies came up, and lost loves and wasted or never-realized abilities…it was all so bloody, in the end, conformist, or if not conformist, then mun-effing-dane. Just mundane and – but, no, it wasn't boring. But was it merely a spectator sport? She could feel the presences around the room waiting for her to come up with an answer. She made a disgusted, angry, unnameable sound that turned all heads toward her.

"Listen," she said. "Listen, all of you. This is my transgression. Pay attention." She didn't wait for them to settle. "I killed my mother." Everybody laughed, especially Jessie-Marie, who couldn't stop for quite a few minutes, a choking sound, without merriment, as if – although it was impossible – she had always known this about Barbara.

"Honestly, Barb," Rosalyn said. "We can always count on you to liven things up."

"Or to make us all look like fools?" Jessie-Marie said, having regained her sobriety.

Sonya said, "Wait. I think…I'm thinking…she means it."

"What? How?" Jessie-Marie asked.

"Or are we speaking in metaphors?" Rosalyn inquired in a conversational tone. *Clearly*, Barbara thought, *she doesn't intend to believe a word I say.*

She knew then, that by saying this she had committed herself and having committed herself, the group would end this night, *and I will die utterly alone.* And soon. Around the room the fluttering increased, she could feel the breath of the presences being held and how such a thing lifted them, bodiless though they were, upward; were they moaning? Did she hear moaning from them? She was not afraid.

"I am not afraid," she told them. Only then did she realize how terrified she was, how terrified she had been for sixty – no, seventy or more – years. Rosalyn's hand had gone to her face, wiping across her mouth and her cheek, before she lowered it again to her lap. Tears were running down Jessie-Marie's face, and losing themselves in the wrinkles and folds, but the light caught them and how they shone, like the miniscule jewels they were. Sonya, dear Sonya, how was it that she liked Sonya best? She did not know, but Sonya's eyes were like two black pools in her pale visage, and for a second, Barbara thought that maybe Sonya had murdered someone, too.

Or were they, all of them, perhaps only one person? One soul?

And what if all the tinkling sounds and the bells, and muted voices up and down the wide, bright hall from which they had isolated themselves were not even real? Could it be that the only reality left anywhere was right here in this room with the spirit-souls gathered around them and the four of them speaking some kind, some version, of something that could be truth – to each other, out loud, into the suddenly stifling air.

"I killed my mother," she repeated stubbornly.

She drew in her breath, listening, asking for help in telling this story and not knowing from whom she hoped to receive help, only believing that if she could get through the telling, help would be around her. "We had quarrelled; she had called me names again: *putaine, whore, slut.* Don't get me wrong – I had earned every one of those names and she went out of my room and down the hall and it was as if I knew exactly how long it would take her to get to the top of the stairs, to lift her foot to take the first step down and I went in a rush. I *rushed* down the hall and I put both hands on her shoulder-blades – she was a little shorter than I was in those days – and I shoved as hard as I could. The minute I saw that she was toppling hard, over, couldn't stop herself, beginning to go down, flailing, reaching out for the handrail, grabbing at the wallpaper, starting to scream – I rushed back to my own room and I shut the door. Very quietly." She paused, breathing deeply through her nose, her breaths so shallow she was beginning to feel dizzy. "I could hear the thumps and crashes as she went down, and I opened my door and went out into the hall to see what the noise was and my sisters came from the kitchen and the front porch at her scream and the banging and my father from the living room where he had been reading the paper. I said as I hurried down the stairs, 'I came as soon as I heard, but it was too late, I couldn't quite catch her.'

"Only my father looked at me as though he knew what had happened, but my sisters were crowding around our mother and my father had to take over, and he pushed them back and sent one to call an ambulance." She was balanced now, on the edge of the big chair, having, without noticing, shoved down the footrest and, tall now, her back as rigid as a fencepost, she clasped her hands together, wringing them. "But I knew she was dead. I swear I heard her neck break. I can still hear it. I have heard it every night for many, many, many years."

The women ranged round the room, the voiceless ones, the

unseen ones, were murmuring among themselves, the whispering was rising, deafening her. Her friends did not speak, until Sonya said, "But to call a girl, your own daughter, such names..." Nobody else said a word.

Finally Rosalyn said, "Barbara. Are we to believe this?" She said it softly, gently, and if Barbara had had a heart she would have cried at the sound.

"I think it is true," Jessie-Marie said after another silence had intervened while the angels in the room let their whispering die away. "Are you sure that you didn't just imagine doing this? That you were so angry that you imagined pushing her downstairs, but in reality, that she merely tripped and fell? Maybe you just didn't save her – if you could have?"

At this, Barbara laughed. Her breath was coming back into her chest and she rolled her head as if her neck were stiff and she was trying to release the muscles.

"That is what my father finally decided to believe. Although I am sure that he knew better. That is what he told the ambulance people who couldn't revive her and what he told the police and in the end, even the coroner. But I know, and have always known, that he knew better."

"Barbara, honestly," Sonya said, pleading. "Surely this is a bad dream only, a wish you had that when it was fulfilled you blamed yourself for. Surely this is not true." Then she seemed to cock her head as if listening; *she wants to know what the angel-souls think*, Barbara thought, and listened herself. But now they were silent.

"I am here to tell you tonight, that when I was seventeen or so, I killed my mother by pushing her as hard as I could down the stairs, and that no one saved her. Not me, not her guardian angel, not anyone. My mother died at my hands." Oh, such a collective sigh emanated from around the room and she half-expected the *presences* to reveal themselves. A very long silence ensued that ended when Barbara raised her hands ceiling-ward.

"Why do they not take me?" she cried. "Why do they make me suffer so? And on and on and on? Can no one forgive me?" But the spirit-souls had gone.

Around her she heard voices, those of her friends and the occasional word registered: brandy, medication, priest, prayer.

SISTERS

Inspired by Anton Chekhov's play "Three Sisters", 1900

THEY HAD GROWN OLD, AND EACH OF THEM LOOKED AROUND EVERY DAY, and said to herself, *how on earth did I wind up like this?* But before too long, in trying to answer this question, their minds would veer first, instantly, to childhood, to puzzle over this or that small incident, then move on helplessly, in chaos, to some other memory, or else to bafflement as to why things had happened in the way they had, and so none of them ever managed to answer the question. Although, at the same time, to each of them the answer was also perfectly obvious until examined – those old assumptions about each of them and about how their family were, under closer examination, turning out to be mostly wrong – resulting in just as much confusion and uncertainty.

No, it was some other question they were asking themselves for, as the eldest, Virginia, sometimes said to her sisters on their annual visit, "That is, how is it that each of us is alone? That's the question," although the other two didn't necessarily agree with this assessment. "It is simply how things are for old women in this twenty-first century." Virginia again, letting out a satisfied grunt as though her statement finished the matter.

"And the twentieth," Melody, the youngest surviving sister, said, shifting on the sofa to nurse her newly-rebuilt hip and steadily sipping her glass of white wine.

"I was about to say, and the nineteenth," Ava, the middle sister, added, and sighed. "But I think families were still families then and didn't they take in their spinsters and widows? So, although it was probably just as awful in its way, at least one lived in the bosom of one's family, and could feel oneself a part of something normal." Ava was given, on occasion, to talking like a nineteenth century novel, rising verbally sometimes even to the height of a Henry James sentence, spieling it out as she gazed high up into space, although more often she got lost in her own sentences' complexities and had to let her voice trail away. Sometimes, though, she made it to the end, maintaining the relationship of the clauses and the phrases, and not forgetting the original idea, at the close, tying a bow on the tail of a subdued snake. Her cheeks would flush at such moments, and she did not look at her sisters, both of whom, if she had looked, would be gazing at her with closed faces and inscrutable expressions in their eyes, which she would have known immediately signified dislike. Maybe even hate? Or merely boredom with her and her airs?

In her youth, Ava had published four small books of poetry, books that had been reasonably well-received, with the critics calling her a 'promising' young poet. When they said it for the fourth time, she had stopped writing poetry and had begun to teach English literature to freshman at the university they had all attended. Occasionally, in those early years, Melody and Virginia had asked her why she stopped writing poems, but she always refused to answer. Privately, though, she felt it was because having four sisters constrained her in the matters about which she really wanted to write, and she disavowed completely obscurity, thought that it was not a kind of brilliance, but instead a dodge for people who didn't know what it was they wanted to say.

So she had stopped writing and gone back to get a Master's degree, specializing, very oddly or so everyone said, in Hemingway. What woman specializes in Hemingway? Even her thesis advisor had asked her this question to which Ava could only shrug: *I like Hemingway.*

"We are like Chekhov," Melody, the romantic one, remarked. It was sad, Ava thought, how often Melody fell into childish sincerity, descending far too often into what Ava and Virginia saw, and shuddered at, as sentimentality.

"Don't be such an idiot," the oldest, Virginia, said. She was the one who could not seem to stop herself from, in the middle of a conversation, letting escape a burst of venom, then tightening her lips and snapping her head away, as if someone else had spoken and, while she deplored it, was above reproving the speaker. That she was a pressure cooker full of steaming rage was evident to Melody and Ava, and had always been, although the source of the rage wasn't clear to them. Virginia had been their parents' favourite, and had gotten all the attention, and could get away with anything, even throwing the most outrageous tantrums to get what she wanted without getting sent to her room without supper or even slapped for being so disrespectful to a parent.

They were the ones, thus, who had reason to brim with rage. But, of course, did not. "I hate falsity," Ava said, rebutting the Chekhov comment, although she was as false as any of them, and knew it, not that the other two would have recognized what she was referring to. She shrugged one shoulder and tried to roll it, saying nothing, but wincing. Once, when she'd been playing football with the other kids on the school playground, two girls pumping up high on a swing collided with her. She recalled the moment the force of the blow turned everything black and then she was on her chest on the ground and her playmates were crowded around her, peering into her face, helping her up. Back in class, she could see their teacher considering sending her home because she couldn't move her arm and, as her friend told her, her face was chalk white. But the incident had happened a long time ago in a faraway northern village on the prairies, and nearly winter, and she would have had to walk home, and maybe the teacher hadn't wanted to let her go alone. Or maybe her teacher was just too young and poorly educated to recognize an injury when she saw one – if there wasn't blood and nobody was unconscious. In those days, homesteading barely ended, everyone had to be tough, Ava told herself as she often had; it was a *cultural imperative*.

Her parents hadn't taken her to a doctor either, though, and for a long time as an adult when the shoulder had become a steady problem, growing worse with the years, she had considered being angry at her parents over this. Then she remembered an almost identical scenario, once again when she and her classmates had been playing a game, their own mixture of football and rugby – they were so remote that nobody knew the proper way to play either game – and she had calculated precisely how and where, if she ran as hard as she could, her trajectory would meet that of the girl running with the ball and had hesitated, thinking, *I might hurt her*, had run anyway, brought the girl down hard, captured the ball and raced away with it, and only then glanced once over her shoulder to see the others running to rescue the classmate she had so efficiently brought down. She supposed, with a mixture of resentment and resignation, even a touch of amusement, that her bad shoulder was her punishment. But then, she was no longer sure which incident had happened first.

It was no use asking her sisters. Melody had been too young then and Virginia had begun to confuse her memories, and, even though Melody and Ava had sometimes been present when an incident Virginia was recalling had happened, Virginia refused to accept their corrections, insisting that, because of this or that, she could remember as clearly as she remembered her own name, that she was right and they were wrong. Melody would sigh and look away, while Ava would gaze at Virginia as if she were a particularly interesting species of lizard, and Virginia, lost in her reconstructed reverie, smiling an inward smile, pleased as heck with herself, never seemed to notice. It was as if she loved the pleasure of her creation more than she loved any kind of truth. But Ava could see the frozen earth with the sparse covering of yellow grass speckled with hard frost. Remembering that playground, the frigid air and the white sky above it, she shuddered, thinking of what cruelty she had once been capable. She wondered about that. Her desire, even as a child, to understand the world, to see what would happen – she hadn't had control of it then. Hadn't understood it. Did she now? *But I am not cruel anymore*, she told herself.

"I need a drink," Melody would say after one of these moments, reaching for the half-empty bottle sweating on the teak coffee table in the southwestern Ontario humidity, and refilling her glass while the other two looked on with careful neutrality. Virginia and Ava would have been happy to drink more, even to become alcoholics in their last years as their grandmother, who died at ninety-six, had been, ("pickled" everyone had said, although not Ava, who deplored clichés), except that Ava had a mild case of diabetes, and Virginia had serious gut problems: bowel dysfunction, and acid reflux barely controlled by her drugs. Anyway, Melody could hardly walk; that was why she drank. "Who could blame her?" Ava would say to her friends when she got back home to the

Okanagan. "With Theo not even recognizing her now and so violent that he has to be in a locked ward and drugged to the gills all the time." Ava was herself long divorced, while Virginia was merely separated, had been for the last forty-or-so years, yet still often spoke of getting back together with Magnus one of these days.

"Which could happen," Melody often said, as Magnus continued to live only a few blocks from Virginia and they saw each other almost every day, although considerably less often now that Magnus had suffered a string of strokes and the social workers were angling to get him into a nearby nursing home. How Virginia would visit him was a mystery. Taxis, Ava supposed.

"We are all terrified," Melody said. Such a quiet voice, so light and delicate. Outside, the rain dripped ceaselessly down the window, and through the glittering haze the sisters could see the enormous fir that took up the entire front lawn, and loomed like death over Melody and Theo's house with its row of leaky dormer windows which the repairmen couldn't seem to fix. "Such a fortune those men make out of helpless old women like us," Virginia often pointed out, and, for once, neither Melody nor Ava contradicted her or objected to her remark. Now she announced, "We need to get out and go somewhere," setting down her glass of ginger ale so hard that it was a wonder the crystal didn't crack.

"Have a canapé," Ava said, passing her the plate. Virginia sniffed as if she were insulted, waving them away. Ava took one and ostentatiously, not looking at her sister, popped it whole into her mouth. Salmon paté on cream cheese, how delicious. She longed for a butter tart from the plate next to the canapés, but knew that if she started to eat them, she would never stop and then her blood sugar would rise unacceptably. It wasn't worth it. She sighed, then coughed to cover it, curling her fingers, and bringing them up against her mouth. Virginia's gaze rivalled the cold disapproval their mother had been able to summon in a second. It said, *such vulgarity*. How she could cow them.

"What time is your plane?" Melody asked. Her sisters said in unison, "The taxi arrives at ten tomorrow morning."

Virginia added, "As you know, we are not taking the same plane because we live in different cities." Melody dipped her chin in embarrassment. Could it be, Ava wondered, that she is getting forgetful like her husband? God forbid, but she had to admit that, nowadays, she was more than a little forgetful herself, and that terrible things happened all the time, so dementia or whatever, for all three of them, was not outside the pale of possibility. And, any day now.

They had once been five. They had paid an older brother no mind, had never paid him any mind, and he and his third wife, a wealthy widow, had gone many years ago to live in Spain. They didn't come back to Canada and their children (who were not their brother's) had scattered across Europe, except for the one who lived in Florida and collected art. The other two sisters had died – Ellen, who had been older than Ava but younger than Virginia, while in her thirties – and Rosemary, the youngest. Both had died of cancer, as had their parents. This was why the remaining three, Virginia, Melody, and Ava, felt the importance of trying to get together at least once a year whether they enjoyed their three or four day meetings or not.

Dutifully each year, they made their arrangements, conferring with each other over several weeks about dates and whose house they would meet in. Since Melody's hip surgery two years earlier, Ava and Virginia had flown to her house in southwestern Ontario, *land of milk and honey*, Virginia, who lived in Winnipeg, never forgot to say, bitterly, as if Ontario had deliberately set out to put her in her place. The previous year they had met in late August, and the heat and humidity had been record-breaking, nearly doing them all in, so that they vowed never again to meet in summer. Now it was mid-October, and would not stop raining. Each of them had begun to wonder why they bothered with these uncomfortable meetings where none of them enjoyed themselves, and the absence by death or desertion – who remembered which? – of husbands, children, siblings, parents, grandparents, aunts and uncles hung like the proverbial lead weight over every minute of every day they spent together.

"Do we even like each other?" Melody had asked her husband, referring to her sisters, but of course Theo had not replied, striking Melody's coffee cup to the floor and splashing coffee everywhere, including across the wall, as well as soaking Melody's pantsuit. Fortunately, it was an old one, a faded brown that she always wore to visit Theo, because you could never predict what he would get it into his head to do. "I'll never get these stains out," she had said to the aide, who had come running.

"Tomato juice?" the aide asked. "Or is that for raccoons? No, I mean skunks."

It seemed, they implied to each other without ever saying so out loud, that they kept meeting because each of them was all the others had left; but Virginia told them out of the blue the morning she and Ava had arrived, three days ago, "For our mother's sake, because she would be devastated if we stopped caring about each other." Ava, doubting this, had offered instead, "To honour her, our mother." She seemed to have dropped the Henry James effort, was edging toward Raymond Carver.

"Admittedly, she cared more for some than for others of us," Virginia spat, staring hard at Ava, and then whipping her head away – Virginia had always liked Rosemary best, not that anyone cared – and tapping the fingers of her right hand angrily against her left arm.

"Does that mean…" Melody began tentatively, after a beat.

Ava spoke quickly over Melody's voice, "Sometimes one, sometimes the other," gaily, as if it were all a big joke. Or was she taunting them? Who knew any more whom their mother had liked the best, and who cared anyway? Melody snorted. She was on her third glass of wine but, when she took a quick breath and tried to speak, Ava interjected again.

"Mother did her best. She wasn't a saint."

"And she had her own mother's influence to contend with," Virginia pointed out. But they had all said all these things a thousand times before, and while they knew them to be true, and that it was pointless to complain now, of the things that had happened in childhood, when they all had one foot in the grave and would soon join their sisters, they still wanted to speak these things, even when they bored each other to death, made them so impatient they could hardly sit still. That remark would always silence any of them if one of them began a complaint about their mother. Their mother had not liked disloyalty, and had drummed into them that disloyalty to family members was a sin and a crime. This rule had not seemed to apply to their father, but that subject was one about which they maintained an absolute silence. They had their doubts about the value of such loyalty, each of them, but still.

Virginia was gazing at the big tree out in the front yard. Ava and Melody never could figure out what she wanted. The rain had let up, but the fir tree was swaying now in a strong wind. Melody had leather sofas, one taupe, which Virginia was sitting on, and the other a mouth-watering cream, which was Ava's favourite, and on which she always made herself comfortable. Melody and Theo had

had money, although the nursing home was probably making quite a dent in their assets. Melody could always sell of course.

"Storm is finally blowing through," Ava remarked.

"Yes, it will just get nice so we could go out somewhere and then you'll be gone." The other two understood this remark to signify how lonely Melody felt with Theo in the locked ward and the kids gone wherever they had gone. And her bum hip limiting her further. Such a misery old age was.

Ava had always preferred her sister Ellen because they had been thrown together when they went to university: their parents would pay for their education only if they shared an apartment. Of course they fought. Ellen, one year older, had way more dates than Ava, seemed unable to settle on even the most desirable boy, always looking for somebody cuter or smarter, but Ava got better marks, except for the time she had gotten a B in Philosophy 101 while Ellen had gotten an A. Ava had barely known Rosemary, or so she always said, because Rosemary had run away with her boyfriend at seventeen, while Ava was working at her first after-college job, and hadn't come back even after the boyfriend dumped her. By then she had a job and an apartment and apparently really liked the folk-music club scene in Vancouver where she sometimes played her guitar, so she just stayed on and had died there many years later, the mother of four grown children, all of whom, since, seemed to have melted into the woodwork. Ava could no longer remember why Ellie had been her favourite sister, and not guitar-playing Rosemary. Ellie hadn't married and had no children so there was nothing left to remind Ava of her. One day, Ava was sitting watching television, and it crossed her mind, for no reason at all, to wonder if Ellen had been gay. What a shock! But she had kept that insight to herself, even when, after that, she thought that maybe Ellen had committed suicide and hadn't died of cancer as their parents had claimed, sending them notes to inform them of their sister's death, and telling them not to come home as the funeral was over and there was nothing they could do. To take such a secret to your grave. She sometimes just shook her head over her parents, as they all did.

"I think the wind is going down," Melody said, as if she were singing. Nobody answered her. Virginia had clicked on the TV. A panel of males in varying shades of blue suits, white shirts, and gently-patterned ties argued soundlessly, laughing with what appeared to be immense enjoyment at each other's wit.

"Mother wouldn't care." Virginia said, but she kept her eyes stubbornly on the screen.

Ava and Melody looked at her. "She's been dead for thirty-five years. Why would she care?" Virginia's tone was growing sharper. "Did she ever say that she wanted us to stick together? Did she ever beg us to stick together? No! She never said a word about any such thing." Silence ensued.

"It's true that she always let us make our own decisions and didn't try to get us to change our minds, even when she thought we were wrong." Melody was near tears. She reached for the wine, but dropped her hand before it came near the almost-empty bottle.

"I wish she had been a little more directive," Ava said. Did she really wish that? "She didn't want me to marry Robert, but she never said a word, and so I married him." In a moment of weakness after Bob's death, she had confessed to them that he had had a mistress through most of their short marriage.

"And stuck with him right to the end, no matter what." Of course, Virginia, always claimed to have suspected as much.

"Maybe she took it for granted," Melody said. "That we would stick together, I mean."

"This is sticking together?" Ava regretted saying this, or regretted what she recognized as fury in her own voice, but too late.

"What else is it?" Virginia snapped. Pursed-lip glares between Ava and Virginia. Neither of them saw the tears that had begun to trickle down Melody's cheeks.

"Don't go away," Melody said. "If you go away, I'll have no one."

"Do you think we have anyone?" Ava asked. All of them were thinking, we have each other, but no one would say it, because really, was it true?

THE DEPARTED

Inspired by James Joyce's "The Dead", 1914 approximately

SHONA, HER GREAT-NIECE, WAS STEPPING PAST THE TODDLER SITTING IN the doorway – Agnes's own great-grandson? Or a neighbour's child? – when Shona's new husband, Tyler, came up behind her, catching her by the waist and nuzzling her neck so that, giggling, half-turning toward him, she lost her balance and, trying to avoid the child who was absorbed in the screeching, light-flashing toy robot he was holding, banged her shoulder and hip against the door frame. She linked her arms around Tyler's neck and kissed him. As if they were all alone in the room. Behind them, in the dining room, women's high-pitched chatter went on, accompanied by the tinkling of cutlery and clink of china as they set the extra-long Thanksgiving table.

Had anyone ever loved her like that? Agnes considered, riffling through her memories of husbands, lovers, and boyfriends from sixty or more years ago. *Oh, probably,* and couldn't stop herself from snorting out of a distant, instantly dismissive amusement. *And yet, here I am.* Small children trotted or crawled past in waves, the older ones stepping over her legs the same way they did over the dog. For safety, the dog had crawled behind the armchair. She eyed the children without saying anything. They weren't looking at her anyway. Her overly-large son had given her the chair of honour again, his deep leather recliner which, even though she was a big woman, was

87

too big for her. He was passing drinks around to the ten or so people seated on the two sofas and the other chairs: a wingback tapestry armchair, several leather-covered chairs – what did they call them? – Danish modern maybe? Or not. Arthur had done well, but, she thought, watching him as he reached her, he is just now figuring out that it might not have been worth quite that much effort. Or possibly what she saw as his evident unease was about something else. Geordie and Sheila Stewart in the same room with his beloved Emma? Why did the Stewarts come, then?

"Have a little wine, mother?" She believed she had nodded. He poured an inch of white into a glass on the table beside her and moved on with his bottles, one red, one white, asking, bending, pouring. People kept arriving, laughing in the foyer, in the living room, banging things – bottles of wine onto the sideboard, elsewhere bathroom doors, even letting open drawers run merrily to noisy stops – someone was clinking unmusically at the piano. A woman called from the kitchen, "Devon, stop that!" Another crash as the piano lid came down. *Roland Somebody-or-other. Such a cliché,* she sighed out loud, *the first boy I kissed.* Emma, Arthur's still-chic chestnut-haired wife of nearly thirty years, came out of the kitchen, her apron smeared with flour and a worried look on her face that vanished the instant a guest called to her from across the room.

"Take a minute, and have a little wine with us." It was Geordie, otherwise known as *the idiot.* Sheila must be in the dining room. Good thing. Sheila hated it when Geordie and Emma had one of their little tête-à-têtes, evidence, everyone knew except Arthur, of the affair they had certainly had a few years earlier. Agnes hadn't herself worried about it; Arthur was not the leaving-your-wife type even if he found out; her own son, but a bit of a stick-in-the-mud. *Got it from me,* she supposed. *I never could move on.* Although she wouldn't have minded being a fly on the wall in the Stewart bedroom when the inevitable discussion took place. Sheila, five foot two and still a giggly blond – some people never grow up – but her style was effective; and, even through Geordie's affair with willowy Emma, she had hung onto him and his money.

Arthur, oblivious as always, must have invited them. No, *determinedly* oblivious. Poor Arthur. She could hardly reconcile the dark-haired, suavely-bearded man with the two-year-old, the four-year-old she had loved with a tender fire for which there was no accounting in the world, as though that love had come before the world existed, and not after.

Roland Frank it was, and they were both twelve or so, after dark, on the small patch of leaf-littered grass in the shadows under the elms, while inside the church hall Father Desmond let the children's choir take a quick break for cookies and lemonade. She couldn't remember much about the kiss; only that it had been hard, not gentle, as if Roland thought that firmness would show the seriousness of his intent, or his capability of going further – his sophistication, that was it. Another dismissive snort. *Did I forget again and do that out loud?* But no one was looking at her. She had a quick glimpse of herself as the black hole in the otherwise overly-bright, busy room. Or, the insensate, inexplicable lump. That's what she was to all these people, who probably weren't even certain whose parent she was. Or was she some large, lonely, old lady taken in by the ever-kind, volunteering Emma?

Emma was chatting distractedly in the doorway, clearly anxious to get back into the kitchen. *I am wry*, Agnes thought; *I am gazing wryly at her.* Once she had been Emma, centre of this moving crowd of Thanksgiving celebrators. How they enjoy telling her *you can't do a single thing; you should rest.* Really saying, *would you please die and get out of our hair. I am now queen of the kitchen; I am now first in your son's heart.* As indeed, Agnes admitted, Emma definitely was, despite everything, whatever 'everything' meant.

She mused on: Hallowe'en. Candied apples. Smoke. Oh, yes. They were in school together, grade eight, or perhaps seven. That falling-down old school in the worst part of town, some of the children the progeny of prostitutes and petty criminals, the rest of them just the children of the Catholic poor. How oblivious one's parents could be. How nakedly stupid. Of course, she didn't exclude herself from this pronouncement, hated to think of all the mistakes she and Alistair had made as parents, even while loving their children and trying their best. Yet she and her siblings had wound up in that dilapidated old school, the radiators knocking out steam all winter long, the windows cracked, and that disgusting old pedophile, the principal. *But she is wearing a skirt!* the girls all said, whispering to each other, their eyes round – they must have been – when they gathered together after he had made Colleen lie on the floor for a first-aid demonstration. What they really meant, though, was that he had made her lie on her stomach while he demonstrated CPR the old way, that slow rhythmic pressing on her back at her shoulder blades. She had the biggest breasts of any of them, and every single one of them, innocents in those days – nothing like the kids today – knew in a queasy, non-explicit way that this was wrong and worse, that it happened intentionally.

She watched the revellers around her, none of them looking back at her, bursts of laughter, the children shrieking at each other. *You didn't tell your parents that kind of thing; you couldn't, you weren't sure what it was that had happened.* Afterwards, Colleen had kept her head bent, her dark hair falling past her cheeks hiding her face, but the back of her neck, even her arms below her short-sleeved blouse flushed red, and she brushed repeatedly at her skirt, not wanting to talk to us. *That old bastard.* He probably wasn't even Arthur's current age though. Fifty or so? She hadn't a clear idea. Older than her parents were then, though.

Two teenagers who she suspected were relatives of hers – she now saw so little of the grand and great-grandchildren she didn't quite recognize the girls – were helping set the table and were taking the pickles out of their jars and arranging them neatly in cut-glass pickle dishes that, empty, could be made to ring like fairy bells and which had been Emma's long-dead grandmother's. What were fairy bells? The loveliest small sound that a crystal dinner bell someone had given her used to make when you rang it gently. What a crash when the cat knocked it off the shelf and broke it. Not so musical then! Jennifer, Emma's sister Angela's daughter, was passing a lacquered tray of canapés, which the men, faces reddening now from drink, took without glancing at her, popping them in their mouths whole, seeming to chew without noticing they were. Jennifer passed her by as if she hadn't seen Agnes. *A steady diet of that treatment when you're old.*

She found herself now thinking of Stanley Raddysh, whose real name was Stanislaus. He had shown her his birth certificate one day when they were walking home from school. Stan. In the days when you could safely carry your plasticized, wallet-sized, birth certificate with you. He had freckles across his nose and cheeks, which, even though she was only a child, touched her by their delicate vulnerability against the fine-grained, pale skin below his eyes. He was a tall boy with light brown hair cut too short. In grade nine his locker had been next to hers and she had said – was it to say something original to get his attention, or was it inadvertent? – "Someone in your house sure knows how to iron," and the other girls had clustered around to admire the perfect way his mother had managed the tiny gathers below the seam of the yoke of his, even then unfashionable, shirt. Imagine remembering that after seventy years. *It is just possible I loved him.* This thought startled her, caused a flood of tenderness in her abdomen, followed by a soft regret in her head. Or in her gut? Although they were often together outside of school hours, she had never kissed him: they almost always met with a pack of other kids. He had had a kind of restraint, a maturity none of the rest of them had. *He might have loved me, if I had...* She could feel – could it really be? – tears prickling at the bottom of her eyes.

Now a couple who had just arrived was coming from the foyer into the living room where the chatter was getting louder as the guests drank more wine or scotch. She supposed the air was full of the roasting-turkey smell. Year after year, more of her sense of smell had diminished until now she smelled very little although, if she concentrated, she could remember the smell of roasting-turkey. Arthur had disappeared, and Geordie was introducing the couple around the room in a casual, jokey way, missing her entirely, at which the woman, who Agnes didn't think she'd ever in her life seen before, for half a second looked faintly disconcerted at this rudeness, but was instantly distracted by the introduction to the next adult, a neighbour, Agnes guessed, no, one of Arthur's employees, judging by how uncomfortable he looked, jiggling his tie as if to loosen it, and still wearing the only jacket in the room. Most food interested her little now; textures, on the other hand, hadn't deteriorated much. She could still feel a caramel candy melt across her tongue and ooze down the trenches of her mouth. No wonder she was so fat. On the other hand, who cared? Even her doctor didn't.

She turned to the middle-aged woman sitting closest to her, somebody's mother visiting from Alaska. Slender and stylish, this one, with a smooth cap of pale-blond hair. Maybe seventy.

"I'll soon be dead," she said comfortably to her.

"Won't we all," the woman said. "I'm Vera, by the way."

"Is your husband here?" Agnes asked, glancing around the room.

"Oh, Bennie," Vera said. "Bennie departed some time ago." Agnes took this to mean he was dead.

"Did you love him?" This was what she loved about being really old. Everybody thought you were just batty, so you could ask whatever question you wanted.

"Does anybody really love anybody?" Vera asked, but she wouldn't look at Agnes.

"I would say yes," Agnes offered after consideration. She spread one hand flat against her sizeable belly. On the other side of the room, three little girls were trying to get the adults to move their feet so they could spread out a paper game on the floor.

"Take it downstairs," Shona said. None of them were her children. "Right now."

Obediently, the children carefully folded the large, marked paper, as if they knew better than to argue, although they probably had no idea who Shona was. Without speaking, they collected the cardboard parts and tucked them under their arms or in front of them, pressed to their flat little chests and rounded tummies. As they walked away, they put their feet down carefully, as if the floor might give way.

"Shona! They don't have to go downstairs!" said blocky Auntie Violet, Emma's older sister, dismayed. She always sided with the kids unless they were punching each other. Violet had no children and Uncle Ross often left for long periods of time. That can't go on much longer, Agnes thought. Ross was ill, anyone with half an eye could see that as he stood, legs crossed, one elbow planted on the fireplace mantle, glass in hand, although apparently no one had. Maybe he was finally getting the long predicted liver cirrhosis. A nasty one, that. Her own first husband, James, had died of it, although not until they had been divorced for quite a few years. The little girls kept moving, getting away from Shona.

"Yes," she repeated to Vera. "It's just that it never seems to last. Don't you think?"

"My point exactly," Vera said.

James had been tall and blond, with a killer smile – that was what all the girls said, that he had a killer smile. Agnes's face felt hot, her cheeks especially. What now? She considered: No, the room wasn't overheated; no, she wasn't running a fever; no, she wasn't angry at anything and she sure wasn't embarrassed. So what? *I was thinking about James's killer smile and then my face felt hot.*

"After James, Alastair," she muttered. "It's Alastair I've lost." She looked around, as if he were merely standing in the other room or out on the deck having a smoke. Loud laughter came suddenly from the kitchen, and a crash as if a chair had been knocked over. Luckily, Vera hadn't heard her.

"I hope that wasn't the turkey," Vera said.

"Whose parent are you?" Agnes inquired.

"Over there." She pointed with an upward jerk of her chin toward a handsome boy of about thirty, who had taken off his suit jacket and rolled up his shirt sleeves. Agnes noticed that ties were coming off, or maybe nobody had worn one. Some new fashion. "He is Emma's nephew Nick." She shifted gears: "Once married – I was, I mean – to Emma's younger brother, Malcolm."

"Oh, my god," Agnes said. After a pause, she added, "Really, who cares?"

"You said it," Vera replied, glancing up at Agnes's face, and then quickly away again. "I have three daughters. I usually spend all holidays with one of them, but Nick seemed to feel he needed to have his mother for Thanksgiving at least once before she kicks the bucket, so I got on a plane, and here I am. Imagine, all that way and the dinner isn't even at his house." She had crossed one slim leg over the other and was clasping her knee with both hands, fingers laced together. Once, when she was a child, Agnes had done that at the kitchen table, but she'd pushed her knee as far from her chest as she could, her hands had slipped, she had fallen forward and banged her face against the table edge so hard her teeth had cut right through her lip. What could anybody do about that? Nothing. She remembered the blood and how frightened she had been.

Her memory took her now, swiftly, to the time *the old bastard* had stood reading to the class in his deep voice, the book open on his palms held chest-high and, as he read, he had moved his hips ever so slowly against the edge of her desk – she sat in the front row – back and forth, back and forth, and she knew that the bulge in his trousers – she could say it now – was his lumpy penis pressed against her desk, and her face and chest not a foot away from it. He rocked back a couple of inches, then forward to press the wood again, and she knew that what he was doing wasn't right. Though she had tried not to, she had stared at the front of his pants, her elbows bent and resting on her desk, chin and mouth covered by her hands. Such a stupid thing, yet for seventy-five or more years she had remembered it; she was still troubled by it. *I am still troubled by it.*

Emma was calling Arthur to come and start carving.

"Turkey's ready."

"Food's going on the table," another woman called, her face

lost behind a steaming bowl of something-or-other. Much commotion, mothers organizing children, adults beginning to move, still chatting with each other, finishing conversations, lagging, nobody wanting to appear too eager, Geordie and his son Dan at the sideboard opening wine from identical bottles. "Should have been opened a half-hour ago," Dan was grumbling, while behind his back his father rolled his eyes to the room. Once she and two of her best girlfriends from school had looked up *the old bastard's* address in the phone book and on a Sunday after mass had strolled nervously past his house. It was snowing, and the whole town settled deeply into its Sunday quiet, with the snow falling so thickly, big soft flakes that spread on their hair and the shoulders of their coats, that, subdued as they were by the sight of the cottage where their principal lived, they could hear the falling snow whispering around them as it fell. As if to comfort them. *What hard little girls we were. But, no, we were not hard at all: We were weakness itself.* She was afraid she would weep.

And the cloakroom – this time her turn in it when the principal was out of the room, as he so often was. A boy kissing her, fumbling at her sweater, the other kids calling, "He's coming, he's coming," and the rush of their footsteps as they tried to get into their seats before the door opened and *the old bastard* caught them. Who was that boy? She knew she shouldn't allow that touch on her sweater, was terrified of getting caught, but – but what? Joey Plamondon, that's who it was. All the girls had crushes on him. *I must have been a sex maniac*, and then, laughing out loud, *at thirteen we were all sex maniacs. Even those of us who didn't know what sex was.* Even as she tried, she could not now make out what to think about that realization. How puzzling it all was. Still.

Arthur was bending over her again.

"Take my arm, mother."

"I can get up myself," she said, suddenly angry, although not at him. As he bent toward her, his eyes fixed on her shoulder rather than her face, she caught a glimpse of something there – her little boy, gone so long ago from her. She touched his face. He moved his gaze to her eyes then, and she saw such – although momentarily only and a shock to both of them – undisguised tenderness in his. For that instant, her breath stopped, she couldn't catch it, getting out of the chair was harder than she thought.

"All these people," she said into his ear, "I'm not sure who half of them are."

"It is confusing," he agreed. She was on her feet now, straightening her dress while he waited.

"Not confusing," she said. "It's just that who they are doesn't matter anymore. Who they are is not relevant to whatever matters now."

He was frowning, thinking, as she knew he often did, that she was batty, or getting there. Roland Frank came back into her mind and then *the old bastard* and the tricks he got up to. Yet hadn't he also brought her forward into life? Hadn't he also brought her here today? Such a mess life was, such a glorious, ridiculous mess.

They stood in the doorway now, he was leading her to the chair at the head of the table where they usually put her, although they then ignored her, passing food around her, filling other glasses while she would sit in silence amidst the noise, eating little, slowly, and thinking of the foolish, precious past.

DOWNSIZING

Inspired by John Cheevers's "The Swimmer", 1964

David and Richard had died, and Lucinda decided to think of her second two – or numbers three and four – Cody Mitchell and Walter Toews, as mistakes. They had been, in the current parlance, nerds when they were all in high school together, so lost in some puzzling self-satisfaction that they had been oblivious to the actual fact of their nerdiness, and, although she had hoped for improvement, they had turned out to be, still, nerds. She had begun with them because they were easy to find, having never moved more than twenty miles from their high school in rural southern Saskatchewan, and because she hadn't thought of them as presenting much of a challenge.

Cody and Walter were quickly crossed off the list she had sat up most of one night compiling, first off the top of her head, and then by consulting her high school yearbooks, then her university yearbooks – she had graduated long ago, in the years when her university still had yearbooks – and then what she could find of her husband Sylvestre's yearbooks from his college in Quebec. After his death two years earlier, she hadn't gotten around to donating them to his alumni society, a lapse in her otherwise efficient organization of the dreaded, but inevitable downsizing project. Maybe she should think of aged Cody and Walter as practice.

She hadn't made a second trip to see Jimmy Sheehan, but went straight from the café where she had met Walter for a thoroughly

dismal lunch – *I mean, how dull and self-obsessed is it possible to be?* –
to Jimmy's law office just down the street in the town of Empire
where they had all attended high school sixty years earlier. Her best
friend from those years, Marnie Massie, who had married a farmer
down the road the day after graduation, kept Lucinda up on the lat-
est news about their old classmates, which was how she knew that
Jimmy's wife was now completely gaga and in a care home. She
knew also that Jimmy had re-opened his law office and that it was
said he was working mostly for oil companies in the area. She hoped
that he would not be like the first two – or numbers three and four –
and reminded herself that the few times all those years ago they had
gone out together had been reasonably pleasant.

Jimmy invited her into his inner sanctum and sat her across his
desk from him as if she were a client, in a wooden chair of the type
that law offices hadn't seen since the nineteenth century. He then
leaned back and placed his hands across what would have been on
anybody else a belly but that on him was closer to a basin, and
waited with an apparently disinterested patience. She would have
recognized him anywhere, but alas, this was not a good thing: still
pale, slight and not tall, still bespectacled and prim. What was it she
had once liked about him enough to put his name on the list? His
calm, she decided. Having herself come from a home always chaotic
with parental disagreement and anger, she had liked his composure
and evident patience.

"What can I help you with?"

"Jimmy, I just came to visit you, I'm not here on business." She
gave him her best smile, turning its full brightness on him, widening
her eyes and willing them to gleam and hold his. "Sorry," he said. "I
don't take regular clients anymore anyway – divorces, wills, property sales, neighbours suing neighbours, that kind of thing." They
made desultory conversation for another few moments during
which, in response to his refusal to engage beyond the most super-
ficial level, she grew irritated and decided to get to the point.

"I understand that you've – to all intents – lost your wife. I too,
have lost my husband. You and I were good friends many years ago.
Do you think we could revive that friendship – I mean, now that
both of us are alone?" Look at the expression on his face, she told
herself: baffled, an urge to laugh quickly suppressed – no, he didn't
suppress it, it died a natural death – and now, he was beginning to
look...she wasn't sure exactly what. "Oh, come on, Jimmy," she

said, no longer hiding her exasperation. It had been a long morning, a long lunch, and now this. "I am not suggesting we sell your first-born, or burn down your office and run for the tropics." He had stiffened and pushed his chair back from his desk.

"Well, gosh, Lucy," he said. "You always were the unconventional one, weren't you?"

She was staring hard at him, trying to find the tiniest spark of interest, which she might be able to blow into a flame. "No," he said. He thrust his chair back the rest of the way and stood. "I cannot imagine what goes on in that head of yours. You always did have nutty ideas about what constituted fun. Always did have to go too far." He had come around his desk to stand pointedly by her chair, so that she rose slowly, and as he kept on walking to his door, opening it and standing there, she felt she had no choice but to follow him.

At the doorway, she resisted the urge to caress his cheek in the faint hope of causing him a stroke. "You have become a narrow man," she told him, still smiling. "I had hoped you had grown more open-minded as you aged, but you have grown more closed."

"You know nothing about me." He put his face close to hers, and his eyes radiated pure malice. "I...never...liked...you," he hissed. "And I like you less now."

"Now Jimmy," she answered gently, as if she were his mother, when in fact she was not and never had been someone to toy with: "You know that first part is not true."

It dawned on her as she was climbing back into her car rental that her old rejection of him still rankled and had, over the years, burned into hate. She hardly knew what to make of his tenacity, and for a minute recognized that perhaps, as a young woman, she had been a bit too casual with the affection of boys like Jimmy. In any case, strike him off the list too. That meant three down. No, five.

When she had told her daughter what she was planning, Julianne was full of disapproval, despite approaching middle-age and being divorced, with no man on the horizon.

"Honestly, Mother," she had said, "What crazy thing are you up to now." It wasn't a question.

"If you don't take some kind of action," Lucinda told her in as reasonable a tone as she could muster, "you will wind up alone, Julianne, and, believe me, when you're old and a woman, that is no fun at all." But Julianne only saw her mother as demeaning herself, and also, Lucinda noticed for the first time, harbouring some sadly delusional ideas about her own attractiveness.

"He will not fall from the sky into your arms. I know this. Just look at the statistics." This, Lucinda had done and the male-female ratio itself, never mind the unattached male-to-female ratio, not to mention the plethora of fifty-year-old divorcées perfectly willing to marry old men, were more than merely disheartening. But Julianne was lost in her complacency, and Lucinda's warning wasted.

"I'm not a bad person," Lucinda had said afterward to her neighbour, Alicia, whose husband had left her as soon as the kids hit university. "My goal isn't to entrap some unwilling male – I'm a reasonable person – it's just to offer them what I want for myself and which is usually what they want, too. Most men don't even know what they want, besides the impossible, and, failing that, to have their dead wives back again. I think I'm doing the only thing that makes any practical sense. In the end, we would both win."

Alicia had shrugged her shoulders and said, "Lord knows I wish I had a partner. If you can pull it off…" She sighed and, switching gears, said, "I'll die of envy." Lucinda had pointed out that there was no reason she couldn't do this herself, but it was pretty clear that Alicia just wasn't into such a thing. It puzzled Lucinda as to why not, but then she had always found people puzzling, now that she thought of it. They seemed to hanker after some mysterious spiritual thing that Lucinda couldn't identify and, as far as she could tell, neither could they. While she knew what would make her happy and was going after it in a forthright and honest way. And, also, at least she knew these men. It's not as if they were on a dating site and total strangers, and one of them might be a psychopath. But Alicia clearly thought her friend's plan was pretty suspect, although when asked, she was unable to tell Lucinda why, any more than Julianne had been able to. Finally, she confessed.

"I called an old, very serious boyfriend about a year after Jack abandoned me. I'd been in love with him, I heard he was divorced, and I just…but I had to drink two glasses of wine first to get up the courage to call him."

"What happened?" Lucinda prompted. Alicia made a face, looking away from Lucy.

"He couldn't scramble away from me fast enough. Told me all about his wonderful new wife, how he had found the woman of his dreams, was the luckiest man on earth, and all that baloney. I could never face the humiliation a second time. It was just too awful."

Adolph, called by his besotted older sisters "Addie" when they were all young, number four on her list – or number six, depending on whether she counted the two who were dead – was waiting at the airport for her when she arrived in Regina, telling her there was no point in her taking the bus or renting a car when he had to be there anyway to pick up some machinery parts. When she had said she would be stranded with him then without a car, he laughed and said he'd make sure she got back to the airport just fine.

They started out by shaking hands, but then she set down her carry-on bag, and, to his evident surprise, put her arms around him, tilting her face upward to kiss the cheek he finally proffered, although she had been aiming for his lips. When she stepped back, still touching his arms above his elbows, she noted that his weather-and-wind-darkened cheeks were flushed, and she wanted to laugh out loud, but also to chide him.

"Didn't we love each other once?" she said, seizing his eyes with her, she hoped, dancing ones. She could see that he still didn't know how to deal with her; his response involved mouth move-ments but no sound until he muttered, "Yeah, I guess so." She picked up her carry-on, linked his arm – he still didn't seem to know that he should crook his and pull her a little closer to him – as he walked her out of the airport and across the parking lot through a thin snowfall to his truck. Oh, those farm boys she'd grown up with. What a sorry lot, she thought affectionately, al-though the best of them steady and strong.

"It'll warm up in a minute," he said, once they were both in the truck. "I just made it on time; had some trouble with a yearling. Fi-nally got him back in."

"Are you still ranching full time?" she said, her tone somewhere between surprise and disapproval. Whoops.

"Didn't I tell you that?" They had exchanged a few short letters before she informed him she was coming to see him.

"You said you were thinking of selling and moving into town, so I thought you had given up ranching. I thought that was why you had time to come and pick me up."

They approached the exit now, and he was reaching through the window to put his parking ticket into the machine. Watching him, she saw the power was still there in his broad shoulders, and the sureness of his movement. Lucinda smiled to herself and relaxed, slipping her hands into her opposite sleeves in what she recognized, with a slight caution to herself, as a satisfied way. She hadn't meant to be calculating, that is, beyond the making of the list, but had to accept that she was being calculating – no, deliberate – in the words she chose to say and the way she said them. But how else to do this? These men were a wary lot who never seemed to know what was good for them.

"We got a long drive ahead of us to Empire," he reminded her.

"The better to get reacquainted," she told him, giving him her twinkling smile, and in the way he smiled back, she knew he was truly glad she had come.

"I got Maisie from the next place to get the guest bedroom ready for you. I gotta admit that since I lost Alice I haven't been the best housekeeper in the world. Maisie cleaned up a little for you, too."

"Is Maisie your girlfriend?" Might as well get to the point. He laughed.

"Don't you remember Maisie Weens? She married Bill Wenzel. Bill's as alive as you and me. She just works out a bit like that to bring in a little cash. Bill rules the roost and, just between you and me, he's a little on the stingy side." They were approaching the edge of the city, and now drove out in the countryside where skiffs of crusted snow rested under shrubs and against rocks.

After a couple of hours of driving, during which she quizzed him about his ranch and what had happened to all the people she had once known, she began to pay more attention to her surroundings. If she had misgivings, remembering the community they had both come from with less pleasure than she was showing, and having forgotten how very long this drive was, she stifled them, chiding herself because, after all, nobody could have everything.

"This is a little hard for a city girl to take in," she said, gazing at the empty, snow-spotted landscape around them, and slid closer to him, pressing against him. He hadn't been her first lover, but close; either second or third. That she couldn't remember the order anymore – David, Walter Toews, Adolph, or was it David, Adolph, Walter? – didn't really upset her. She hadn't really been a promiscuous girl, just one all the boys were after. It led to opportunity that possibly she should have let pass. She was aware that the truck had swerved a little into the left lane.

"Icy this morning," Adolph said, not showing any alarm, and

she relaxed again, even allowing herself to rest her head against his wide shoulder. "Nearly there," he added, and gave her that smile again. Warmth had settled into the cab that wasn't coming from the truck's heater, but from the two of them together, and she thought contentedly, turning her face into his worn, canvas sleeve: Maybe him; maybe he is the one at last.

Later, she would remember that next Adolph had said to his truck, "Whoa-oa-ohh," and then they were in the ditch and rolling over and over, first cab over tailgate, and then again, and then sideways, and then bang, she saw a wall of yellow grass patchy with snow – somebody screamed – coming at them – she would say afterward, again and again, "If I hadn't done up my seatbelt ..." until someone, Maisie, she said she was, a face that Lucinda thought she knew, said, "Shshsh, Lucy; it's all right now," but tears were streaming down the woman's face as she spoke. "You hit the approach; that's a deep ditch and you skidded and rolled and slid, full force, blam, right into Wojinski's approach."

After the emergency ward and a sling placed on her arm, Maisie tried to take her home for the night, but Lucinda insisted on staying in the town's only motel, telling her that she was too upset to be with people, which was true, and that she needed to be alone. When Maisie came the next day to check on her, and, as her bruised and twisted body was half-killing her, making it impossible just yet for her to ride a bus for four hours and then a plane for another four, she agreed to wait, and attend Adolph's funeral, hard as it would be, and indeed was.

She didn't know what to make of Maisie's remark she had overheard at the funeral that "Adolph must have been off his game," until she realized that he hadn't done up his seatbelt, and besides that, a countryman, he should have had no trouble handling an icy road. She felt ashamed and even guilty, as if she had caused his death, and that perception warred in her with the one that said she was being ridiculous: the accident was hardly her fault. And all those strangers at the funeral looking sideways at her, plus his now-bulky sisters treating her as if she were from Mars, and evil itself.

Afterward, lying sleepless back in her own apartment in Hamilton, where she had moved after Sylvestre's death, her French not being good enough to stay without him in Montreal, Adolph's face and his touching yet thoroughly masculine shyness hovered around her every night, enough to make her wonder if he was haunting her because she had killed him. She couldn't stop herself from thinking: so much for number four – or six. She had reached the end of her high school list. Now, as soon as she could muster the strength to do it, she would tackle the university list.

Lucinda had easily recalled the names of boys she dated in university, but found locating them harder because, once they had obtained their degrees in engineering or economics or medicine, they had moved all over the place. Then she had to find out if they were still married or not, or if they had live-in partners. Merrett Jacoby's name came up. He had taken her to her first freshman dance, and what a lovely boy he had been: smart, good-looking, and mannerly, a full cut above the old high school crowd, back in Empire. She tracked him down in Denver, of all places, instead of the more likely Calgary or Vancouver, where he had retired from his own engineering consultancy business, and found out by trolling the obituaries and death notices in their alumni magazine that his wife, Myrna Snow, was long dead and that he hadn't re-married.

Considering how best to approach him, she decided to phone him to tell him she was planning to holiday in San Diego, and, having a five-hour wait in Denver between planes, had thought to see if they might meet 'for old times' sake'. She felt a bit guilty about this minor deception, but then, how else to re-invigorate her relationship with him, if indeed it would be possible. She reiterated to herself that she didn't intend to break up a marriage or even a relationship. She simply wanted to be married again, and to someone she could love, or at least enjoy living with. She was willing to engage in minor deceptions to achieve this goal.

On the phone, he sounded happy to hear from her, and, when she landed, was waiting at the arrivals gate. It took them a minute to recognize each other: He had only a fringe of white hair left around his tanned skull, and now wore heavy, dark-framed glasses, but he was still good-looking, and he had bothered to put on a tie, sports coat, and pressed trousers, as well as shined and elegant loafers. She could see he had done well in life. He put out his hand to shake hers, as the others had done. As with them, she pulled him close to her for a hug, and as the others had done, he acquiesced.

"You look quite marvelous, Lucy! You haven't put on a pound. However did you manage that?"

"You don't look as if you've put on any weight either," she said, gazing up at him admiringly.

"I'm still running and going to the gym."

"At seventy-five?" She couldn't hide her surprise. They were both a few years older than seventy-five, but he didn't correct her.

"You bet," he said. "Myrna put on a lot of weight and her heart quit when she was only sixty-five. I'm not going to let that happen to me." He led her toward the row of restaurants and shops near the airport's glass entrances. When they were seated in the dark hush of what appeared to be a good restaurant, and he had ordered wine, she said, "So you never married again?" He shook his head, no.

"Bachelorhood has been good to me," he declared, looking at her and laughing, with a touch of sheepishness that she found, well, charming.

"I can see why," she said, using the upturned face, the steady, bright gaze again. She had never been an eyelash batter – so embarrassingly obvious – and wouldn't start now.

He shrugged. "Whatever," he said. "I like women. It was tough there, at the end, with Myrna. She couldn't seem…" He paused, turned his face away to look across the nearly empty room. "She couldn't seem to be happy."

"Some people are like that," Lucinda said. "Just born with a burr in their britches." They both laughed.

"I haven't heard the word, 'britches,' in many years," he said. "Tell me about your life. I heard you married a Frenchman."

"I did," she said, nodding, "and he was a great husband. That's why I want…" here she hesitated, embarrassed at enjoying herself so much she was forgetting to be vigilant, then, her turn to shrug, "to marry again." He had been buttering a roll, and now his motions slowed; he cut the roll in half, and then in half again, as if he were solving an engineering problem.

She said, cheerily, but not trying to hide the wry note in her voice, "It seems to be getting chilly in here." He gave a little, not-unfriendly, snort without looking up. This was going all wrong, and she found to her sorrow that she didn't know how to fix it. Damn! And he was so clearly what she was looking for.

He looked directly into her eyes, "I've found that having women as friends works best." She could feel her face flushing, her whole body was heating up, and she fiddled with her earring. Could it be? He was adding her to his list!

"Denver and Hamilton are a long way apart," she told him, refusing to meet his eyes. "It's unlikely I'll be this way again. Especially given our ages."

"Now, don't be that way, Lucy. I feel about sixty and the doctor says I'm in great shape. Look at you! You look fabulous! We could have a great time together. Change your ticket, and we could drive through the Rockies. Lots of nice inns tucked away in them." She could imagine the inns, and the women he had already taken to them. She was collecting herself now.

"It sounds wonderful," she told him, lowering her voice, and projecting warmth into it. This was now all about saving face. "I'm afraid not this time, though. From San Diego I'm flying up to Vancouver. My granddaughter is graduating from university and I wouldn't miss that for anything." She could see he wasn't fooled.

"I think you're missing a fine opportunity. At our age, how many of these do we get? Think of the fun we could have together." Fun? Did that mean sex?

"Merritt," she said. "I am not a promiscuous teenager. I want to be married, or at least, to live with a partner. Affairs I don't need. They do more harm than good." A long silence ensued, during which the waitress set the plates before them. They had both ordered pasta primavera, and occupied themselves eating and sipping their wine.

She flew back home again the next morning and, for a while, didn't even look at her list, although she knew very well that Garth Whitney, also widowed and living in Victoria, was the next name, and after that she had only two more names to consider. If none of them worked out, what would she do? Give up, come home and live alone, and get used to being old, she told herself, and for a moment felt lost in her downheartedness. She could see her chances dwindling and dwindling again, and she wondered if she would even be able to muster the old charm to make a dent in Garth's inevitable barriers.

They had dated in third year, and indeed, had made love many times, and had talked about marrying, but he had another four years in medical school, and she knew very well that if she married him she would have to support him – that's how things were in those days – and the very minute he graduated and became a full-fledged doctor, he would dump her, worn out by then from her secretarial jobs and running the house and children, and marry the first good-looking young nurse he ran into. Everybody knew medical students were especially notorious for doing this. It had seemed to her, in those days – *I always did have a calculating streak*, she recognized now with some surprise – that she wouldn't choose to engage in this battle, if in the end she would likely lose. And that after years of poverty while he finished his degrees and then went into a speciality. The kids would be teenagers before she had a minute to call her own, and then she would be left alone. Thinking of this, she kept putting off phoning Garth.

But one morning, when she woke and the sun was shining brightly into her bedroom lighting up the furniture and pictures, and songbirds were chirping away in the cherry tree outside her window, she thought, *damn it! I'm going to give it one more try.* Garth had always claimed she had broken his heart, so, remembering the awful Jimmy Sheehan, she decided to phone him first, and to be as direct with him about this venture as she was about it in her own mind.

"Garth, is that you?" when he answered the phone. "This is Lucy Moreau. I was Lucy…"

"Lucy Sutherland!" he said, so eagerly that she laughed. "It's wonderful to hear from you after all these years. What's up?"

"Do you know that Sylvestre died, that I'm widowed now?"

"No," he said. "I'm sorry to hear that. How long have you been alone?"

They had a lively conversation, as if nearly sixty years hadn't passed since the day she had walked away from him, and yet, unlike Jimmy, he seemed to hold nothing against her. Together, they decided that she would come to Victoria to visit him.

Now, on the plane to Victoria, remembering her neighbour Alicia's unhappy attempt to reignite a flame with an old beau, Lucinda had to admit that if the truth were told, she was getting a little tired herself. Feeling her age, anybody else would have said. This last winter had taken something out of her that she didn't feel able to get back. She had fallen ill with a bad flu after the Adolph thing, weeks passed before she was well again, the sling having been long since discarded, and then after the Merrett debacle, her hair had started falling out, and she had finally managed to find a too-expensive wig, which matched her own beauty-parlour blond perfectly, and which no one would ever know was a wig. Still, needing the wig somehow dampened her spirit. She cleared her throat a lot, too, not that it did any good, as the new, unpleasant-sounding rasp would not go away, nor would the pain that came and went when she swallowed, and no matter how much cream she put on her hands, she could not get that new gnarled, aged look to go away. Now her doctor thought she should have a couple of hearing aids. *I mean, really,* she told herself, setting her jaw.

Now, Garth, who was number what? Six, or was it seven? Truthfully, number eight or nine – could it really be that she had been through so many men? But she had to admit that he was one of those who had mattered most to her, whenever she allowed herself to think of her past.

She flew to Victoria a full day earlier than the day she she told him she'd arrive. Beside her usual trip-weariness, the time difference between the two cities was three hours, not to mention the difference in climate, all combining to leave her achy, thick-headed and tired, and it was imperative that she not meet him in that condition. A good night's sleep in a better hotel still did wonders for her skin, and some expertly-applied makeup would bring out the brightness in her blue eyes and the beautiful shape of her full mouth. Shrunken a little, but nevertheless, exquisitely-shaped. She knew that if she didn't look her best at least for the first week or two while he remembered that as a girl she had been full of life, funny, charming – the beauty queen with the winning personality, the yearbooks had said of her – all hope would lost before the relationship had begun. So she gritted her teeth, and put every ounce of feminine expertise into their first meeting.

He met her at his door leaning on a cane – she hadn't expected that – and wearing fleece-lined plaid slippers. He still loomed over her though, and his bulk, in that lovely masculine way, had increased with age, so that for a second she felt like a little girl gazing up at her grandfather. The illusion passed when he spoke, though, in that same rich voice, and that gentle manner. "Lucy," he said, softly, and before she could move he was leaning down, kissing her full on the mouth, so that she lost her breath, and nearly her balance – another of her abilities which had been deteriorating at a mildly alarming rate. "Come and sit with me on the sofa."

It was late afternoon and a gas fire burned in the polished white granite fireplace. Across from the sofa stood a glass wall and then a balcony and beyond that, Victoria's inner harbour with all the sailboats, launches and even a few small yachts. A gilt tray holding a carafe of dark-gold liquor and two matching crystal glasses rested on the coffee table before them. "Before we have dinner," he said, pouring them each a little. She didn't like to tell him that strong drink now wrought havoc with her digestion; she accepted the glass and they touched them together for a toast to their reconnection. The sound of the two glasses meeting, though, was more like that of a tiny crystal bell that seemed to ring something new into the atmosphere, or to signal something she couldn't know. She half-wondered if she were dreaming.

"How are you, Garth?" she asked. "Do you still practice at all?" She had meant medicine, but he glanced over his shoulder at the grand piano. Had it been there when she entered the room?

"I play a little every day, although my fingers are getting stiff. I couldn't live without music." She became aware now that music was playing softly in the background: a string quartet, although she couldn't name the piece or the composer.

"I forgot how well you played," she said. "What a joy you were to listen to. I forgot that completely." He was smiling at her, a gentle, almost fatherly smile, although he reached out like a lover to take her hand, and place it in his large one, cupping it softly with the other.

"How beautiful you were as a young woman," he said. "I was never joking when I said I loved you, or that your departure from me broke my heart. I would never have left you."

Outside the window, dusk was approaching across the gleaming water; the light in the room was deepening. In the dimness, it seemed to her that he was looking younger by the second, that he was the old Garth she had loved when they were young. "I was just amazed by your iron will," he said, laughing a little, as if she were an amusing child. "Do you think now that you made a mistake leaving me?" He was teasing her; he still loved her: to her surprise, she knew that she loved him, and always had, and for an instant, she was consumed by a longing for what she had never had but might have if she had been less determined.

"I think," she said, pleased to hear that the touch of an elderly croak had smoothed itself out; her voice was that of a young woman, full of girlish innocence. "I think that I probably did." She was about to start telling him how now they might begin again, but he interrupted, speaking as if he had read her mind.

"Some things can't be fixed," he told her, touching her hair where it framed her cheek. He was leaning toward her again, his face coming closer and closer, and in his eyes, which had turned dark in the softly-shadowed room, she could see – what was it?

Outside the glass wall the sea breathed long exhalations, rising and falling, its moving surface gleaming like polished sheet metal in the last rays of light.

"At night I dream of the prairie," she told him.

"Your hands tremble," he said.

But he was growing smaller. She reached out to stay him, but he retreated as she reached.

He had begun to fade too; what now seemed to be only a thin depiction of him, never a flesh-and-blood man, was dissolving before her.

What did you come for? a voice she thought was Garth's asked. She wanted to answer him, but just as when she reached for him he had retreated, her reasons, once so clear and strong, were slowly evaporating and she couldn't formulate them; she saw now they had never been anything more than will-o'-the-wisps, both their lives so tiny and inconsequential, mere dust motes in a background so deep, so vast...

ACKNOWLEDGMENTS

I owe a huge debt to the writers whose stories, plays and poems inspired me. My first reading of many of them going back to my days as an English and Art major at the University of Saskatchewan starting about 1957. My stories are, I know, a pale shadow of the brilliance of their work, work that has haunted me all these years.

But times change, lives change, focus changes, and one day a writer sees those stories in a new light, wants to say more, wants to say 'and' and 'but' and 'if,' and a new set of stories emerge. That 'writer' is me, now thinking about, for instance, what might have become of the young woman in "Hills Like White Elephants," or what epic trip an old woman might take instead of swimming across the county as in "The Swimmer," or having discovered a different view of love than that in "What We Talk About When We Talk About Love." This is an old woman's view, seasoned by fifty-plus years of experience since, as an awed teenager, I first read many of these works.

I owe my excellent editor David Margoshes a thousand thanks for, among many other things, helping me to anchor my stories. Thanks to Coteau Books for publishing (for most publishers the dreaded) collection of short stories, my fourth. And after forty years of writing, what does one owe *the muse?* Labour, gratitude, faithfulness. Thanks also to my agent Marilyn Biderman for her expertise and advice.

"The Departed" was originally published in *Grain*, Vol. 45.3, Spring, 2018

"Grace's Garden" is to be published in the on-line magazine, *Joyland*, in early 2019.

ABOUT THE AUTHOR

SHARON BUTALA is an award-winning and bestselling author of both fiction and nonfiction. Her classic book, *The Perfection of the Morning,* was a #1 bestseller and a finalist for the Governor General's Award. *Fever*, a short story collection, won the 1992 Authors' Award for Paperback Fiction and was shortlisted for the Commonwealth Writers' Prize for best book (Canada and Caribbean region). Her novel, *Wild Rose*, also with Coteau, was published in 2015 and was shortlisted for the W.O. Mitchell Book Prize. Most recently, she published *Zara's Dead* with Coteau Books in 2018. Butala is a recipient of the Marian Engel Award, the Saskatchewan Order of Merit, and the 2012 Cheryl and Henry Kloppenburg Award for Literary Excellence. In 2002 she became an Officer of the Order of Canada. She lives in Calgary, Alberta